S E R P E N T I N E
E N I G M A

To Lynne & Ann
Best Wishes
Always
3/3/18

SERPENTINE ENIGMA

CHARLES DOMINA

Mill City Press, Minneapolis, MN

Mill City Press, Inc.
322 First Avenue N, 5th floor
Minneapolis, MN 55401
612.455.2293
www.millcitypublishing.com

ISBN-13: 978-1-63505-109-4
LCCN: 2016907722

Book Design by Robert Harmon

Printed in the United States of America

CHAPTER ONE

It was a bitter and moonless night in this, the winter of 1529. The lone horseman pulled his cloak up to cover his face, in order to ward off the humid, misty, bone-chilling cold. The rushing and icy waters of the Loire were black and forbidding as the rider guided his mount along its banks, skillfully avoiding any misstep which would have sent them both into the abyss. The journey had been a long and torturous one. The agonizing hours had passed slowly and exhaustion for both man and beast had begun to set in. The traveler knew, by instinct, that his destination was close and strained through the black gloom to detect a sign that the end of his journey was near. His spirits were uplifted and he gave a silent thanks as the orangey- red, flickering flames of the lanterns, suspended in the darkness, at the entrance to the chateau, came into view. As he drew closer, the massive, stone structure of the building revealed itself. He pulled up on the reins and stopped before the entrance. A small, side door opened and a man appeared, beckoning him, with a gesture, to enter the grounds. He waited for what seemed like an eternity, but, it was only a matter of minutes until the main gate opened allowing him to pass through. Upon entering, the rider dismounted with great difficulty, fighting stiffness, pain and weariness from the long ride. The horse was stabled and the visitor was taken to a room for a night of welcome and much needed rest. After being given something to eat and drink, he drifted off into a deep sleep, darker than the night through which he had traveled.

At dawn, he was awakened by the creaking of the heavy wooden door at the entrance to his quarters. It opened partially, but, no one entered.

"Who is it?", he called out in annoyance, as he rolled over, the haze of sleep still clouding his mind.

"I've come from the kitchen sir, with some food", answered the meek, female voice, waiting beyond the door for permission to enter.

He sat up and pulled the covers around himself, as it seemed as cold in the room as it was outside.

"Yes, yes, come in", he responded gruffly, still not having fully recovered from his arduous journey and knowing that he was about to embark on another.

The housekeeper came in, set down the food and some wine and lit the small fireplace at the end of the room.. As she was leaving, she advised the visitor that, upon finishing, he was to ready himself for his trip and go to the courtyard to receive his instructions as to carrying forth the mission for which he had been beckoned.

He was ravenous and made short week of the bread, meat and wine left for him. After readying himself for the task ahead, he hurried to the courtyard, as instructed. The day was bright and even though cold, was a vast improvement from the previous night. He approached his horse, which was showing agitation and an eagerness to leave the restraints of the chateau with the steam of its breath issuing forth from its flaring nostrils like some sort of equine dragon and which had been saddled and bore bags of provisions for the journey before him. There was a small figure of a man, dressed in robes, standing next to the large beast and holding a leather pouch. He kept his head slightly bowed and his face was obscured by the shadow cast from the large hood which he wore. As the traveler stood next to his mount, in anticipation, the hooded figure stepped toward him, handing him the leather pouch and speaking to him in a soft, almost imperceptible, voice.

"Take this pouch and secure it with your life, for it has in it a vessel which contains a relic most rareand irreplaceable. You are not to open it, under any circumstances, but, are to deliver it with utmost dispatch. Go west, following the river to its end. When you reach the coast, hand your priceless cargo to someone who will take it to sea and to its final destination, a place of which not even I have knowledge. You have been carefully chosen for this task because you are known to be a dedicated and honorable man. You must swear that you will do all that I have told you, exactly as I have told you."

"I swear on my honor and to God."

"Then, go."

With that, the horseman secured the pouch to his saddle, mounted his steed and began his journey to deliver the mysterious cargo.

As he rode to the appointed destination, the words spoken by the monk rang through his mind.. *What was the relic? How could it be so precious that he must protect it with his life?*

The gravity of the mission weighed heavily upon him as he rode with great haste, taxing both man and beast. Upon reaching the harbor, the horseman gave thanks and a prayer. The ship's captain presented himself. The word was spoken and the relic surrendered. The horseman stood watching as the ship cast off, its sails unfurling in the wind as it made its way to the open sea.

On this day there would be no answers, only a mystery to unfold in the future of humanity.

CHAPTER TWO

Finally, the week was over and it was a beautiful, sunny Saturday morning. Geneticist Dr. Joanna Russo was sitting at the kitchen table of her Manhattan apartment, reading the morning paper, listening to the sounds of the city and just generally enjoying the luxury of doing nothing for the next few hours. Like everyone else in the city, she was still profoundly affected by the horror of 9/11, but, she was moving on with her life although she personally knew a couple of those who had lost theirs on that fateful day, a few years before. She was a person of passion who bore a controlled but lingering hatred for those who had committed that atrocity and anyone who sympathized or collaborated with them There was none of that so-called closure for her, nor would there ever be. Most of all, there was that a gnawing feeling of helplessness which, to her, was the most disturbing, emotional residue of the experience. Still, on balance, it was a good time in her personal life.

Ten years had passed since earning her Doctorate in genetics, from Cambridge and, all things considered, she was doing quite well. Best of all, she was living in the city in which she had grown up and she reveled in its sights, sounds and frenetic twenty four hour activity. Her life was focused on her work and uncomplicated, without personal entanglements and she was free to plot her own course, blissfully ignorant of the events which would overtake her and change that life forever.

She was interrupted by the last sound that she wanted to hear, that annoying tone indicating that someone was at the door.. "Now what?", she grumbled as she walked stridently across the room to answer it as if to confront some perceived adversary standing on the other side. She swung the door open and immediately calmed herself after being greeted by the pleasant and familiar face of Grace, the mail carrier, pen poised in one hand, the other holding a letter.

"Sorry to step on your Saturday morning Doc, but, somebody in England wants to get hold of you real bad."

Odd, thought Jo as her thoughts immediately were directed to Fiona Clark, her best friend during her college days. But, she had spoken to Fiona last week, so, that was unlikely.

She signed the receipt and Grace handed her the envelope.

"Thanks Doc. Have a good weekend."

"You too, Grace."

Jo closed the door behind her and glanced at the envelope as she walked back to the kitchen where a half cup of lukewarm coffee was waiting. The envelope was nothing unusual. It was a white business envelope, obviously containing a letter. The only things remarkable were the Cambridge postmark and the printed return address, "The Serpentine Foundation", below which was an unusual symbol. She sat down, took a sip of the coffee and hastily ripped open the envelope. She unfolded the letter and saw that, like the envelope, it bore the letterhead and the symbol. It read:

> *"Dear Joanna*
>
> *I write you today, not as professor to student, but, as one colleague to another. I have followed the progress of your career and have waited until now to contact you, because, it seems, our research has begun to run on parallel tracks. I invite you to join me and promise you opportunities and revelations that will challenge even your imagination.*
>
> *If you accept my offer for an initial meeting, I will, of course, provide transportation and accommodations. If you decide to join my Foundation there will be substantial compensation.*
>
> *I encourage you to accept. You will not regret it. That, I promise you.*

*Please contact me to confirm, one way or
the other. If you agree, we will arrange a time
and date.*

Cordially.

Ian Slattery"

The letter was a complete surprise and unusual in its
informality. It was a sales pitch, out of the blue, designed
to create interest, yet empty in detail. Jo reflected how
out of character this was for Slattery who had been one of
her professors during her studies at Cambridge. But, then
again, ten years had passed and things change.

She put the letter down, intending not to deal with it,
at least for now. But, it was distracting and no matter how
much she tried to ignore it, she kept coming back to it. How
strange and unexpected and why now? After all, she had no
contact with Slattery, either on a professional or personal
basis, since she graduated. She stopped herself from
becoming too analytical as to the why's and wherefore's of
the matter. Perhaps, this was a gift horse she was looking
in the mouth and a little positive rationalization might be
the order of the day; carpe diem and all that sort of stuff.
It sounded like a challenge with a little bit of the unknown
thrown in. Even though she did love New York, maybe
a temporary change of scenery would be therapeutic.
She could simply get a leave of absence and lock up the
apartment for a while. She would square things away with
Slattery, call up Fiona, her college buddy and best friend
to announce that she was coming to Cambridge and

make arrangements. What the hell, if the Slattery deal fell through she could still spend some time in England, the Amalfi Coast and maybe even explore her roots in Sicily. How complicated could it be?

CHAPTER THREE

The bright light streaming in, woke Jo up. The passenger, in the window seat, had opened the shade. She felt awful. She always felt awful waking up on a trans-Atlantic flight after too short a sleep. There was the usual movement up and down the aisles as passengers squeezed past each other in futile attempts to reach the lavatories, quickly. God, she thought, *why doesn't someone invent a way to beam you from New York to London?*

"Breakfast?" the flight attendant dutifully asked, with the pleasant and practiced smile of those in that profession. She could hardly bear the smell of the re-warmed eggs and ham or bacon or whatever it was, much less even consider eating the stuff.

"No thanks, just coffee and a bottle of water."

Jo spent the remaining couple of hours relaxing, occasionally speculating as to what was awaiting her in Cambridge and briefly fending off an annoying and overly chatty, middle aged business man, the same passenger who opened the shade and let the light in and who insisted on making advances. She closed her eyes, effectively ignoring him. Mercifully, dawn was breaking, indicating that they were not far from the English coast.

After some time, her rest was interrupted as she heard the power on the engines cut back and felt the plane begin to descend. Shortly thereafter, a member of the flight crew indicated that the plane was in its final approach and made the obligatory announcements about seat belts, seat backs and tray tables. The pilot increased their rate of descent and she heard the familiar low pitched whine of the flaps being deployed and the thump of the landing gear being lowered and locked. Finally, she thought. After a few maneuvers they touched down on the runway, with a jolt. She had made it to England. Now, it was off to Cambridge to meet up with Fiona and find out what lay behind Slattery's cryptic letter. She would spend the night at a hotel and meet Fiona the next day.

It was August in England and unusually warm, even for that time of year. Ten years had passed since she attended University and obtained her degree in genetic research. It seemed like a very long time ago. Now she was being beckoned by one of her former professors to join him is some research project. It was an unlikely turn of events.

It was a long ride from Heathrow to Cambridge and the hotel would be a welcome sight. Upon arriving at the hotel, she checked in, went directly to the room and didn't bother to unpack. She would leave that till tomorrow when she went to Fiona's. Right now all she could think of was a shower and a bed. She gave Fiona a call and got the answering machine. She left her friend a message to meet her, tomorrow at the Anchor for their unofficial reunion. Having made the requisite phone call announcing her arrival, she showered and collapsed on the bed to spend the rest of the day and night sleeping herself back to normality.

The next morning, she was feeling refreshed and anxiously anticipating meeting up with the woman who had been her closest friend during and after college, even though an ocean separated them. She left the hotel and walked over to the pub, finding a suitable table at which to await the arrival of Fiona.Relaxing on the terrace of the riverside pub, she took in the surrounding spectacle of the terming masses of young people still on holiday, her mind in a total state of tranquility, in the warmth of the afternoon sun. Listening to the sounds of the voices around her all melding into a kind of soothing white noise, interrupted only by the gentle splashing of water and the occasional sound of wood knocking against wood from the punts being poled lazily down the river was just the therapy she needed after two years of solid work. Her thoughts were awash with pleasant images of past times spent on and about the Cam. Suddenly, a familiar voice transported her back to the present.

"Jo, welcome back!"

It was Fiona, exuberant as ever; a person of boundless energy in whatever she did.

"It's good to be back", responded Jo, as the two exchanged a warm hug.

"So tell me", quipped Fiona, how was the flight? Any body try to light up their sneakers?"

"No, actually the flight went well. The only thing that looked dangerous was the food. Speaking of which, I could use some."

"How about a two ploughman's and a couple of pints of bitter", suggested Fiona.

"Good and we can get caught up. I'd like to get your take on some things and try to get a feeling for what's been going on around here."

Fiona detected a serious tone in Jo's words, but, decide to ignore it until they could catch up on personal matters, over lunch. As they left the riverside terrace and climbed the stairs leading to the pub, it was easy to see why they had always been considered the odd couple by their fellow classmates. They were a study in contrasts. Fiona, a sandy haired wisp of a woman, small in stature and slim, yet strong in spirit and constitution, rarely slowing down long enough to take a deep breath before rushing on to the next project. Jo, on the other hand, was tall, dark and Italian, giving the impression of being laid back, but, actually less than even tempered when provoked. Her striking looks never went unnoticed, many times to her annoyance. She was a scientist, serious in her profession and it was often hard to drive that point across to those with whom she dealt. Both women were imbued with an iron resolve, in all that they did, and a fierce loyalty to one another, which would serve each of them well and be tested, as events unfolded.

They entered through the open large wood and glass doors of the crowded pub, Fiona asking Jo to stake out a table while she braved the food line. Finally, tray in hand, and after battling her way through the hoards of international teenagers milling about and who crowd the pubs during the summer months, Fiona made it back to the table.

"Some things never change", Jo reflected, gazing down at the familiar, cheese, bread and pickled onion, occupying her plate.

"And some things do", commented Fiona. "But", she continued, "we can go into details later."

The two friends did some catching up even though they tried to keep in reasonably regular contact with each other. The conversation then turned to the primary reason for Jo's presence in Cambridge.

"It's great having you here, but, I'm still curious as to who or what could pull you away from the big city on such short notice. Your e-mail didn't go into any detail."

"The who or what is Dr. Ian Slattery."

"Ah, the good Doctor. Haven't you heard? Oh, of course you haven't. How could you. The consensus is that Slattery's gone over the top. In fact, some believe that he's a bit bloody mad."

"Ian Slattery, the mad doctor?" Jo showed a combination of amusement and skepticism at the suggestion.

"Wait!", exclaimed Jo. "Before we get into any more of this, I'm going to need another bitter. Care for one?"

"Please."

Jo went to fetch the drinks, returned and the two exchanged a belated toast in celebration of their reunion. She continued the conversation.

"I know the message was vague. I couldn't give much detail because I really don't know what's on Slattery's mind. I was surprised that he was no longer associated with the college."

"Well, it wasn't much of a surprise around here", Fiona responded, "I'm not privy to all the details, but, my understanding is that the good Doctor went off on his own and engaged in some independent research. The college administration felt he violated professional guidelines and was in conflict with university policy and protocol. It was all very hush, hush."

"He always pushed the envelope", observed Jo.

"That's true. But, this time, rumor has it, he was pushing it legally and ethically."

Fiona's revelations were disturbing as she continued to relate more of the facts.

"When he fell out of grace, it wasn't long before he moved his operation, whatever it is, to the country. He settled on a large farm, about a half hour drive from Cambridge, to continue his work. It's now more of a compound than a farm.. We call it the Area 51 of Cambridgeshire, although you don't get shot for getting too close. At least not yet. But, enough about that. You'll be seeing for yourself, soon enough. So, you're the expert. What do you think Slattery's up to?"

"I'm not totally sure. He did make some reference to his interest in my present research."

"Which is?"

"Genetic memory."

"That sounds a bit edgy. Let's go back to the flat. You can fill me in on the way."

The two downed what was left of their drinks and left the pub. As they strolled along the path which passed the "backs", the extensive and serene pastureland which lay behind Kings College, Jo reflected on the peacefulness of the moment, but, could not help her mind wandering in speculation of what the coming days would bring. She felt an inexplicable and vague yet palpable anxiety. But, for the moment, she would enjoy the familiar and comforting surroundings with Fiona and explain events leading up to her arrival in Cambridge. Fiona broke the silence.

"So, fill me in."

"You know that two years ago I took extended leave from the government and hooked up with a private institute to do some experimentation that was going into some interesting areas."

"I remember that you had told me something along those lines."

"One of the things they were working on and which fascinated me was the idea of genetic memory. The theory that more than instincts could be passed on from generation to generation. That, in fact, learned behavior or memory, at least at a primitive level, could actually be inherited. This would change a lot of thinking in the scientific world and I couldn't pass it up.'

By this time, Fiona's analytical mind was working overtime and trying to construct a logical scenario from what her friend was telling her with what she had heard about Slattery. It was much like one of those huge jigsaw puzzles with hundreds of pieces laying all over the table. Fiona could only put together a small fraction of one of the corners which was not enough to identify even a hint of the entire picture. Anyway, she thought it was best not to jump to any conclusions. There would be plenty of time for that, later.

"Actually", continued Jo, "it's not as sexy as it sounds, What I did was to duplicate a somewhat obscure experiment that found that certain, simple learned responses, in a type of worm, could be transferred to the next generation, without further behavioral conditioning."

"Well, it's doubtful that Slattery got you over here to train worms," observed Fiona.

As the two continued to make their way to Fiona's flat, Jo pulled a folded piece of paper from her purse and handed it to her friend.

"This is what I received from Slattery."

Fiona proceeded to read the letter.

"And his brought you back over here?"

"This plus a plane ticket, plus a healthy salary offer and accommodations near the Foundation, if I want. I'll stay with you, as we arranged and commute to the lab. That gives me some independence and privacy and a place of retreat until I find out what this is all about. I don't know who he has hooked up with, but, money seems to be no object."

"You sound as if you have some trepidation."

"I have some reservations, but, nothing serious that would make me pass up the opportunity. You know, professional curiosity."

"Didn't curiosity kill the cat?"

"Not this cat."

They picked up the pace and arrived at the flat. It was beautifully done and was a restful and inviting place, on the second floor in a small, new apartment complex constructed of red brick, nestled out of sight on a small back road on the edge of town, right on the Cam and overlooking the serene and beautifully landscaped gardens of one of the colleges across the narrow river. True to form, Fiona already had her luggage delivered from the hotel.

She was scheduled to meet with Slattery, at his compound, on Monday. But, it was Friday and Monday was far enough away so that the two friends could indulge themselves in a weekend of relaxation, shopping, afternoon tea and maybe some pub crawling. For now, she would put her concerns on hold.

CHAPTER FOUR

Monday arrived. The anticipation of the day's events acted as an internal alarm clock and Jo was awake at sunrise, eager to start the day, not lingering in bed in spite of the early hour. She went over and opened the drapes to check the weather. It was bright and sunny; a perfect day for a drive in the country even if it had to be combined with work. As she exited the bedroom into the hallway, the aroma of freshly brewed coffee filled the air. Not surprisingly, Fiona was already up and about, doing what had to be done to move things along in anticipation of their trip to the Slattery compound.

"Are you up yet?", called Fiona.

"Coming", responded Jo as she walked down the hallway and into the kitchen.

Fiona was in the process of pouring two cups of coffee. There would be no traditional breakfast tea, for, as British as she was, she couldn't stand the taste of the stuff.

"Well, good morning Dr. Russo. Have you prepared yourself to meet up with your colleague, today?" There was a hint of good natured sarcasm in her voice.

"Ready as I'll ever be."

Fiona placed the coffee and a rack of toast on a tray and took it out to the balcony where the two enjoyed a leisurely breakfast and discussed the plans for the day.

"What time are you scheduled to meet Slattery?"

"Noon."

"Good. That'll give us the whole morning and plenty of time to get out to the compound."

It was agreed that Fiona would drive to the compound in order to give Jo some influence as to the duration of the meeting and provide an excuse to terminate it, if need be. She felt that, until she had some feeling as to what would be asked of her, she wanted to keep as much control of the situation as possible.

Eleven o'clock rolled around and they decided to leave even if it was a bit early. This would give them time to take a detour and enjoy a leisurely ride through the country.

They walked downstairs to the garage and Fiona opened the door, revealing her brand new Jaguar XKR drop top. Her love of fine cars and addiction to Formula One Racing, provided an interesting counterpoint to her otherwise practicality.

"Nice wheels and British racing green, of course", commented Jo.

"Of course."

The two jumped into the car, put down the top and roared off to their destination.

As they wended their way through the narrow streets of Cambridge, they noticed that the vacation crowds were already thinning out and the city was returning to its normal routine as the Michaelmas Term for the colleges drew closer.

They sped along the winding country roads, neither of them saying a word, but, simply enjoying the moment. Fiona was absorbed in her driving and Jo reflected on the contrasts of the area which had always fascinated her and which were unlike anything that she could experience in the States. They passed an old pub which had been converted into a Chinese restaurant, but, which still had standing in front of it, the heavy timbers of the old gibbet, a gruesome reminder of the days when public hanging was a spectator sport. The landscape was a crazy quilt of villages containing quaint thatched roof cottages, hundreds of years old, interspersed with modern residences of an unremarkable nature. There was the occasional modern institutional building, usually belonging to the University, which might be in close proximity to a small working farm. It was harvest time and they passed fields where crops had been cultivated by horse and plow, for centuries and were now being cut by huge modern machines and over which clouds of pollen were suspended in the air, forming a golden mist, turning the scene into something out of an Impressionist painting. A mile, or so, down the road, the field may not contain crops but, rather, dishes, cameras and the sensor arrays of radio telescopes searching the heavens trying to answer the ultimate questions. Who are we? Where did we come from? Why are we here? How ironic, she thought. These scientists were trying to find answers to those questions by scanning the universe and she and others like her were trying to find similar answers by studying the smallest building blocks of life. Which instrument would provide the answer, if an answer could ever be discovered, the Hubble Telescope or the electron microscope? What was going on behind those fences and walls, she thought. For that matter, what was going on at some of those isolated farms? Did this placid, rural scene hide a sinister underbelly? It was certainly a place where someone who wanted to engage in unorthodox scientific activities could hide in plain sight.

They took a sudden right hand turn off the main road and onto what wasn't much more than an old carriage path, lined by hedges on each side. Luckily, Fiona had been paying attention to where they were going and had followed Slattery's directions.

After they had gone about a mile, they approached the entrance to the compound. It was surrounded by a ten foot chain link fence and although she couldn't see them, her first impression of the premises led her to believe that the compound was also protected by cameras and motion detectors. There was a small, light gray plaque, to the right of the gate, bearing the same name and symbol as the return address and letterhead that she had received from

Slattery. On the gate itself was attached a white sign, with large, bold, red lettering, bearing the obligatory warning:

"NO UNAUTHORIZED
PERSONS OR VEHICLES
BEYOND THIS POINT"

It was a decidedly unfriendly place, but, she was not surprised.

Fiona stopped the Jag about twenty feet from the gate. There was a panel containing a callbox with access from the driver's side. She, rather than Jo, would have to announce their arrival. She pressed the button and waited for a response.

"Yes?", the voice at the other end inquired.

"Dr. Joanna Russo here to see Dr. Slattery."

There was a prolonged silence

"Proceed", the voice curtly ordered.

The electronic gate opened and they entered the grounds.

Fiona drove the last hundred yards and stopped in the driveway of the sprawling old, one story, farmhouse which was hidden from the road by a large stand of chestnut trees. Jo scanned the grounds and saw a group of small, neat, brick buildings of recent construction which looked like they might be residences; probably staff quarters, she concluded. Just beyond the brick structures there were two additional, white, single story buildings. One was of wood construction, L-shaped, with windows. The other, a large square, building, which looked to be built of concrete, as best she could tell, windowless and monolithic in appearance. These were obviously the laboratory buildings. Both had small structures next to them which, she surmised, held backup generators, not unusual for such a facility. But, why two buildings and why the striking physical difference between them if they were for the same general purpose?

While Jo was preoccupied sizing up the place, Fiona noticed the front door open.

"Here comes the welcoming committee", she remarked.

Jo turned to see a man coming down the walkway, towards the car. He was young, in his mid to late twenties and could best be described as about six feet tall and thick bodied, but, not fat, with a closely cut crop of black hair. He was a large man, very powerful looking with one of those body types that starts with a nineteen inch neck and continues down with all of the contour of a fire hydrant. He had on casual clothes, a black turtle neck and slacks, over which he wore the obligatory, white lab coat which, she thought, was more for show than a reflection of his duties at the compound. He impressed her, not as a scientist nor technician but, rather, as one of those over-sized, beefy types who stand at the doors of trendy, New York night clubs, selecting those who enter and those who do not.

"Good afternoon, I'm Doctor Joanna Russo, here to see Doctor Slattery."

"The Doctor's been expecting you. And you Miss?"

"Fiona Clark, Doctor Russo's friend."

"Follow me, please", the surly looking young man ordered in a decidedly Yorkshire accent.

His manner was brusque and uncivil and he did not actually greet them nor did he introduce himself. They did, however, recognize his voice as the one on the security intercom. He certainly wasn't the type of person one would have thought to be associated with Slattery, in any capacity.

"I didn't think that Slattery was in the business of hiring body guards", commented Fiona.

"My thoughts, exactly", responded Jo, as they both got out of the car.

They followed him up the walkway and entered the farmhouse. The sight that greeted them was far from what they had expected. It certainly did not look like the inside of any English farmhouse that either of them had ever experienced or imagined. The parlor was furnished in what could best be described as retro, mostly consisting of chrome, glass and leather, predominantly white and black with floors of highly polished parquet with an ample supply of modern artwork bedecking the walls and providing just the right amount of color. The place was, obviously, professionally and very expensively done. It was certainly a far cry from Slattery's old digs, the rooms he occupied at the College during his years as a professor. Jo and Fiona exchanged glances, each harboring the same thought. What was Slattery up to, where was he getting his money and why?

"Please have a seat. I'll fetch Dr. Slattery." And with that, the assistant disappeared through a door leading to the back of the house.

For a brief period, the two friends were alone but, for now, each of them felt that it was best to say nothing. It was likely that the walls had ears.

They had hardly settled in when Slattery burst through the door and was as animated and exuberant as she had remembered him from ten years ago. He was in his mid fifties, with thinning hair, light brown and graying and a receding hairline, exposing a generous portion of his forehead giving him that intelligent look. He was tall, over six feet and thin and when he walked he took long strides with a stalking sort of gait. He had brilliant, blue eyes that were intense, taking in everything around him and which seemed to look right into your mind when he spoke to you. Jo was an avid Sherlock Holmes fan and Slattery, in appearance, thought processes and mannerisms, always reminded her of the descriptions that she had read and seen in sketches, of the great detective.

Slattery took Jo's hand and clasped it in both of his.

"Joanna, welcome back to Cambridge. I cannot tell you how delighted I am that you accepted my invitation."

"I'm delighted to be back and look forward to the opportunity, Doctor."

"Please, it's Ian."

"Ah, Miss Clark. I see that you two are as inseparable as ever. May I get either of you some refreshment?

Jo and Fiona declined.

Slattery turned to his assistant, who had been standing near the back door, motionless and expressionless, hands folded in front of him as is he was controlled with a switch, which had been turned to the "off" position.

"That'll be all Jack. You can go."

With that, "Jack" left the room. He was still an enigma, but, at least they now knew his name

After some small talk about the last ten years was exchanged, Slattery suggested that Jo accompany him for a look at the facility where she would be working should she decide to come aboard. Fiona was invited to come along, but, she decided to wait in the house while the two went on their short excursion.

There was a white golf cart waiting out front and the two got in, commencing their bumpy ride to the laboratory buildings. During the short ride Slattery was rambling on about the benefits of joining the Foundation, but, Jo wasn't really paying attention. She was concentrating on observing all she could about the place in order to be able to make some assessments and arrive, at least, to some basic conclusions. She felt it odd that no one was about and that the only two people she had seen, so far, were Slattery and his assistant. Perhaps the others were all busy at work in the lab buildings. Perhaps.

The golf cart, with its two occupants, passed by the concrete lab building. Jo could see that it had a steel security door with a covered box attached to the wall next to it, probably containing some sort of electronic device requiring a code for entry. She thought it best not to inquire about the building, at least not for the time being.

Slattery stopped the cart in front of the L-shaped building and they went in. Jo got the opportunity to look around and was introduced to the twelve lab technicians who were working there. They were a mixed bag of Asians and Middle Easterners with a couple of Brits rounding out the group. She was, however, more interested in what they were doing rather than who they were. There was the usual collection of standard lab equipment and test animals; nothing out of the ordinary. Certainly, nothing that would give rise to the exciting possibilities suggested in Slattery's letter.

"Your technicians seem to be doing some work as to in vitro", she observed. "That's not my field." She was short with him in her comment. She didn't want Slattery to feel that he could intimidate her as her former professor. As he, himself, pointed out, they were now colleagues and the student-professor relationship was a thing of the past.

"You're absolutely right", Slattery responded. "You'll be working over here", as he led her to a separate area of the building which was furnished with empty tables and nothing else.

"You can customize this area as you wish. Just submit an inventory, to me, of whatever you need. I hope that my preparations don't seem overly presumptuous."

She did think that, but, kept her thoughts to herself.

"You're probably wondering what it is that we actually do here."

"You're probably right", Jo responded.

"Ah, I see that you haven't lost your sharp tongue", observed Slattery, with a slight grin. He continued.

"Briefly stated, we're doing genetic modification in animals, hence the in vitro fertilization work, that you observed.. Right now our research is in the embryonic stage, if you'll excuse the pun, but, our ultimate aim is to attack world hunger by enhancing reproduction and certain characteristics of growth and quality of the animals that provide us with our food source, at all levels. So, while conventional science concerns itself with extending the shelf life of tomatoes, we're in the business, you might say, of building a better chicken. With this as our goal, there's much international interest and we've been able to attract all of the money that we need and for that matter, all that we want."

"But, if you're aware of what I've been doing in the field, you should know that this isn't my area of interest or expertise", Jo exclaimed with some puzzlement.

"No, no, no", responded Slattery, waving his hand. "What you see here is what attracts the funding for our operation. We also reserve the right to use a portion of these funds, as we see fit, for optional projects. We've chosen genetic memory to be one of those optional projects".

"Enter Dr. Joanna Russo."

"Correct."

"How far have you progressed?"

"No further than you, actually. But, I want to proceed on the premise that two heads are better than one. I want you to reproduce your previous experiment as a starting point and we can go from there. The agreement between us will be simple. You will work for the Foundation for as long as you want and for this you will be paid two thousand pounds per week. We will include a car and accommodations, if you wish."

Jo knew that the offer would be substantial, but, the amount, quoted by Slattery, was much more than she anticipated, in fact, disturbingly so.

"That's more than generous of you."

"Think nothing of it my dear, we can afford to be generous."

At the house, Fiona was taking the opportunity to do a little looking around. She had the uncomfortable feeling that she was being observed. Visions of Jack skulking quietly about or sitting in some sort of command center and watching the monitor of a hidden camera, ran through her mind.

She paced the parlor, feigning impatience, all the while scanning the room, trying to be as nonchalant and inconspicuous as possible. As she walked past an archway which led to an adjoining study, her attention was drawn to a computer which had been left on and which still had something up on the screen. How odd she thought as she observed that it was not in English but, rather, in Chinese. She could recognize it. Unfortunately, she was unable to read it. Was it left on due to lack of concern as the contents would disclose nothing, or, was it carelessness? She turned her attention to a bookcase, noting that it contained a curious mix of volumes dealing with genetics, Renaissance Art and New Age topics. An odd assortment, she reflected, for a man with Slattery's professional background.

Her concentration was abruptly broken by the sound of a golf cart pulling up to the front door. Jo and Slattery were back.

"That was quick", remarked Fiona as the two came through the door, engaged in animated conversation concerning Jo's possible association with the Foundation. She walked away from the entrance to the study and towards them, hoping that Slattery was too distracted to notice that she had been in proximity to the archway and that she had a clear view of the computer.

Jo turned to Fiona. "I think we're ready to go."

"All set", her friend responded.

"I'm glad that you chose to come, and I'll look forward to your decision", Slattery commented, to Jo, as he escorted the women out to their car.

He turned to Fiona and gave her an insincere smile. "It's been a pleasure Miss Clark.

No doubt I'll be seeing you again."

Her instinct was that he did not like her and considered her a possible obstacle in the way of luring Jo to the Foundation. It didn't matter. The dislike was mutual.

They left the compound and turned onto the main road back to Cambridge.

"How'd it go?", inquired Fiona.

"Interesting."

"I'm all ears."

Jo described her meeting and its details and what she was, ostensibly, hired to do.

"The man certainly has turned into an enigma", she observed.

"Yes, but, a very well financed enigma", countered Fiona.

A couple of miles down the road they were passed by a black Land Rover going the other way. Fiona saw that the two occupants were of Asian extraction.

"Chinese I'll bet", she blurted out.

"What?"

"Chinese. The people in the Rover that just passed us. I'll bet they're on their way to see Slattery."

"What makes you say that?"

"I saw some Chinese language text on the computer screen in Slattery's study while you two were discussing things at the lab."

"That could explain the source of the funding. But, what could be that important to draw in the Chinese interests or, possibly, the Chinese government?"

"When does Slattery expect your answer?"

"By the end of the week."

"Good. That'll give us some time to do a little bit of research and see what we can find out about the Foundation and the good Doctor's, apparently, very important work."

CHAPTER FIVE

It was Tuesday morning. Jo was wide awake. In fact, it had been a restless and mostly sleepless night. She wanted, on the one hand, to accept Slattery's invitation to work at the Foundation, but, on the other, there was something troublesome about the whole thing, although she could not quite put her finger on it. She lay in bed, staring up at the ceiling and reviewing her options, over and over again, trying to focus on some decision.

The phone, on the night table, next to her, rang loudly, jarring her back to the here and now. Fiona grabbed the call in the living room. Jo listened and could faintly make out Fiona's end of the conversation and was unable to hear who she was talking to or what she was talking about.

"Jo, it's for you", yelled Fiona.

"Who in the hell could that be?", she muttered to herself. It was time to get out of bed and get on with the day and she wanted to know who it was, before taking the call, so, she made her way to the living room where Fiona was waiting, receiver in hand and smirk on her face.

Jo gave her friend a quizzical look, asking, without speaking, as to who was calling.

"It's Petah", Fiona indicated, in an exaggerated English accent, as she stretched out her arm to hand the phone to Jo.

Jo balked at taking the call and put her hands up in front of her as to wave off having to take the receiver. She knew, however, that it was too late, that Fiona indicated that she was there and that she had no choice but to talk to Peter. She also knew that, on the other end of the line, was Peter Simpson, her one and only love interest during her student years at Cambridge. But, that was a long time ago. The flame had died while they were still in university and even though they had kept on friendly terms, when still in Cambridge, they had gone their separate ways. They had not been in contact, with each other, for the last ten years. So, what was this call about and how did he know that she was back in England? Their conversation was brief and Jo felt, awkward after all this time. Peter was insistent that they meet for lunch that afternoon. Jo was reluctant, but, he pressed the point and she agreed. It wasn't so much that she was anxious to re-establish any relationship with Peter, even on a very limited social basis, in fact, she really didn't think that they would have much to talk about and wanted to avoid being thrust into an awkward situation. It was the subtle urgency that she detected, in his request, that made her feel that she would be letting him down, in some way, if she did not meet him. And she could never let Peter down, no matter how long their estrangement. Jo finished the very brief conversation and handed the phone back to Fiona.

"So?"

"I'm meeting Peter this afternoon for lunch. He's driving in from London."

"How did he know that you were in town?"

"He mentioned he was in Cambridge, in a taxi and saw us walking from the pub the day that I met you, but, was late for a meeting and couldn't stop." She shrugged her shoulders and raised her eyebrows in a gesture of skepticism.

"Well, I'm listed in the book, so there's no mystery how he got the phone number."

Jo had agreed to meet Peter at the old wine bar, just off King's Parade. She left the flat and as she walked the winding streets, she was oblivious to the things and people around her. She could only think of yesterday and her trip to the Foundation and now, the call from Peter, like Slattery, someone from her past with an imperative to see her. Why Peter's sudden interest after all this time? The fact that she was, physically back in England was, certainly, not the answer. Peter had made no effort to contact her since they had graduated. How did he really know that she was in England? Was it a coincidence of being in the right place at the right time or something more? Why did he bypass pleasantries during their telephone conversation and press for a meeting on such short notice? It was all so sudden and so strange. Were all the events of recent past connected? Her thoughts changed her attitude in meeting Peter from one of having to fulfill a self-imposed obligation to one of heightened curiosity, eagerness and some anxiety. What was all of this really all about? Within the next two to three hours, these questions would be resolved.

Jo arrived at the street level entrance and walked down the staircase to the bar. It was as she remembered. The bar was combined with an informal restaurant and was pleasant and bright with light shining in through the small windows against the pale yellow walls, contrasting the dark wooden furniture and bar, typical of such places. It was a place where she had many memorable moments with Peter and stepping through the archway, which led into the main room of the bar, was as if she was transported back in time.

As she looked around for Peter, she noticed that the business lunch crowd had left and that it was that time of the day when the place was virtually empty. She spotted Peter at a back table, in an isolated corner of the room. She had butterflies in her stomach, but, wasn't sure if they were caused by seeing Peter, again, or the uncertainty of what was to come.

"Jo, I cannot tell you how wonderful it is to see you again", exclaimed Peter as the two gave each other a hug.

A warm feeling rushed through Jo and just for one extended moment, it was like ten years of separation were washed away. She stepped back and looked at Peter.

"I almost didn't come, but, I'm glad I did. It's been a long time, Peter."

"Yes, it has. Too long."

On her way to the meeting, Jo had wondered how she would feel on her meeting with Peter. They had been lovers and were successful in maintaining a friendship after the passion dissipated, but a lot of time had passed since they had seen each other. It was comforting to see him again and he was outwardly warm and cordial, but, there was no doubt that something, in him, had changed. There was a certain detachment. He was not the Peter that she had left behind in Cambridge some ten years ago. All the questions that she had asked herself started racing through her mind again.

"I've taken the liberty of ordering a couple of Clarets. I hope that's all right."

"Fine."

"Peter", Jo started, but, was interrupted by the waitress.

"Your wine, sir."

"Thank you."

They each toasted their reunion and Jo immediately picked up where she had left off.

"Peter", she repeated, "It is delightful seeing you again, here, like this, in the old wine bar, but, every bone in my body tells me that we're not here to rekindle our romance or reminisce about the good old days. So, why are we here?"

"That's my Jo, right to the point as always", Peter said with a smile. "Then let me get right to the point, as well. You're right. We aren't here for a romantic interlude. We're here because of Ian Slattery."

There was a pause as Jo put down her glass and leaned back in her chair, narrowing her eyes as she glared at Peter and reflected on the suspicions that had run through her mind upon receiving his invitation.

"What about Slattery?"

"We want to know what he's doing, how he's doing it and why there seems to be outside international support for his work."

"We?"

"Let's just say, for the time being, interested parties in the American and British governments."

"And you?"

"I work for the interested parties on this side of the pond."

"Then you didn't just happen to see me walking with Fiona and this meeting wasn't the result of chance."

"Bastard" was the term which went through her mind, at that moment. Her instincts were right about Peter. He certainly wasn't the man she knew ten years ago or, maybe, she really never knew him at all. Did she want the meeting to continue or did she want to get up and leave, turn her back on the whole thing, whatever it turned out to be and head off to Italy with Fiona? She sat, contemplating her next step. Finally, she broke her silence.

"I'd like some honesty here, Peter and I'd like it now."

"Of course. I can't blame you. I'm sure my revelation came as somewhat of a shock."

"How did you know I was in England?"

"We've been monitoring Slattery's mail, what little there is of it. He's a hard nut to crack, but, I suppose that he thought his letter, to you, was harmless enough and he will be right if you decide not to help us."

"If you think he's doing something illegal, why don't you just crash the gate and raid the place?"

"Because we don't have anything but suspicions and he's cleverly connected himself internationally so that any drastic action might have negative political implications. No. We've got to get the goods on him, first."

Jo's eyes darted around the room. She became uncomfortable with the nature of the conversation and having it in a public place.

"Should we be talking about this here?", she asked Peter.

"Don't worry. We pick our meeting places carefully, spontaneously and never meet in the same place twice. As for myself, as far as the outside world is concerned, I'm just another government bureaucrat, no license to kill and I don't even, as you Americans say, pack heat."

"And you have no problem telling me all this which, I would assume, is classified?"

"No. Frankly, we don't have a choice, as you're our best and maybe only chance to get to the bottom of Slattery's activities. Besides, we did a thorough security check on you."

She felt displeasure at the disclosure that she had been the target of a secret security check led by her old boyfriend. It was more than displeasure. She felt violated.

"I knew it", she muttered to herself, in an almost imperceptible whisper. She reflected on the feeling that her instincts had given her, assessing Peter as being cold and calculating. She was right. Peter had been trained well for whatever it was, exactly, that he did in this new life that she knew nothing about.

"Excuse me. Did you say something?"

"No Peter, nothing, nothing at all."

He certainly was not the Peter of old and any vestiges of their previous relationship were as dead as dead could be. It was a real blow to the gut that Peter saw her as nothing more than a means to an end. But, she'd be damned if she'd let him know it. She collected her wits about her, mustered up her fortitude and by sheer mental strength, moved past the momentary emotion.

"Why do I figure in your plans?"

"Because, so far, you're the only one, outside of Slattery's circle, who has the opportunity to access the compound and get close to him. That's also why it was worth the risk to approach you on the matter. He obviously needs assistance and pretty much burned his bridges in England. He also couldn't bring in scientists, even if they had the expertise, from suspect or unfriendly countries, without turning the heat up on himself. You, being out of the loop and involved in research similar to Slattery's Foundation, are the one he turned to.

"What about surveillance? You know, satellites, wire taps, cell phone intercepts and all the rest of it."

"No good. Satellites don't show us any unusual activity. His communications tell us nothing and we believe everything is done by courier, simple and primitive, but, invulnerable to high tech snooping. We've tested surrounding soil samples, checked for radiation and unusual electro-magnetic impulses and even did some limited thermal imaging.

"And?"

"Nothing. The activity is consistent with what he presents to the public. And as I said before, we can't be heavy handed because of political implications. To the world community and those who supposedly advocate the interests of developing nations, the good doctor is somewhat of a hero."

"How much do you know?"

"Right now, only what he's chosen to reveal to the general public. We know that he's involved in reproductive research and genetics associated with food production."

"That's it?"

"Not quite. We have information that he deals with companies and individuals associated with the Chinese government which, of course, implies the Chinese military. But, if he is involved in clandestine activities, they're restricted to the compound and any contacts with others are restricted to face to face meetings at the compound. It's a very effective technique if you don't want what you're doing found out. The compound, itself, though a private facility, and not really having any official standing, has been given a pass and has taken on the aura of an embassy because of its heavy international involvement. The agency I work for feels that it's been given too much autonomy, but, we don't run the government. As to the compound itself, the ownership of the farm and the source of funding involves layers of corporations that stretch from Jersey and the Channel Islands to Macau and Hong Kong. Now, with British influence greatly reduced to practically nothing and Chinese control over that part of the world, we've run into a brick wall."

Peter's comments brought back images of the Rover that passed Fiona's car as they were returning to Cambridge from the meeting with Slattery. Then she recalled Fiona telling her that about the Chinese language text on the computer in the study of the farmhouse. The facts seemed to fit together, but, their meaning remained unknown.

"How would all of this work?", she asked.

"You simply continue as your doing. You live with Fiona, accept the position with Slattery and gain his confidence. Apparently, he's at some stage of research, we can deduce, that it's in your field of genetics and your most recent area of research, genetic memory. He needs someone to collaborate with and you're it. He's started taking chances out of necessity and that works to our advantage."

"And what about Fiona?"

"I repeat, you change nothing. Any deviation might draw suspicion. There is some likelihood that anyone working for Slattery will be watched. We can't be sure, so, we have to take precautions."

Her mind swirled. She had to discipline her thoughts and fully grasp what she was about to do and its implications for her and for those around her. If she was in danger, might Fiona also be put into danger? And was she prepared to deceive her dear friend by not telling her all that would transpire? That would be the hardest part of it all.

The two sat at the table, in silence, Peter staring at Jo and she looking past him, her eyes in a distant stare while she considered her answer. Suddenly, Cambridge was no longer the quaint, friendly place that it had been, a mere couple of hours ago.

"Why should I do this?", demanded Jo.

"I can't give you the specifics that you want because I don't know what you'll find. All I can say is that if the Chinese are interested, it isn't a small thing, either for England or America. We need your involvement because Slattery broke all the rules and took a tremendous chance in contacting you. For whatever reason, he's determined that you're indispensable for him to accomplish his end. This puts you in the unique position of being the only one on our side who can get to him."

"How do I keep Fiona out of it?"

"You can't, not now."

She had an almost impossible choice to make. To decline would, in her mind, be irresponsible and bordering on cowardice. She had never in her life failed to make a tough decision or face down a challenge. But, to accept would require her to lead a double life and lie to Fiona, something which would have never crossed her mind prior to this moment. Then there was Slattery. Even though he may be engaged in nefarious activities, which was nothing more than an unproven suspicion, she would be called upon to breach the trust of a man who she respected, professionally and who taught her much of what she knows. All of this forced upon her by a man who she once had feelings for, but, who now had become the stranger sitting across from her. But, she knew that she would have to make a decision based on principle as she had always done even if that decision would prove to be the lesser of two evils. She thought of New York, the place that she loved, how it had been scarred and her inability, as an individual, to do anything about it, now or in the future. Perhaps, this was a stroke of fortune. Perhaps, this would change all that.

She sat on the edge of her chair and leaned forward placing her elbows on the table. Her eyes were cast down, in thought and she was motionless save for her very slowly running her finger around the rim of her wine glass, her gaze hypnotically transfixed on the shimmering ruby liquid it contained. Peter stared at her intensely as if trying to read her mind or, in some way, attempting to influence it by sheer strength of will.

After some moments of contemplation, she looked up at Peter, but, still said nothing. They sat there looking eye to eye, Jo cupping her hand on her chin and Peter who instinctively looked back at her, expressionless as he was trained to do so as not to reveal his emotions of the moment.

Finally, she broke her silence.

"Alright", she said, in a determined tone of voice.

"That's my Jo! I knew I could count on you", exclaimed Peter in a burst of controlled exuberance, reaching across the table and clasping Jo's hands in his.

"I'm famished. Shall we order?", asked Peter as if the preceding discussion, with all of its grave overtones, had never taken place.

"Sure."

"Another Claret, perhaps?"

"Yeah and ask her to leave the bottle."

Peter smiled, in amusement, at her request.

During lunch, there wasn't much in the way of conversation except for Jo filling in Peter as to what she had seen during her meeting with Slattery at the compound. He knew of Jack, whose full name was Jonathan Dempsey, a man who had some past minor scrapes with the law, but, had managed to elude incarceration. He was a curious choice for an assistant to a scientist but, perhaps not, under the circumstances. One thing about him to keep in mind was that he had allegiance to no one and served the highest bidder. Peter was interested in the fact of the Chinese material that appeared on Slattery's computer and the Asians, probably Chinese, in the Rover. But, this information was not very revealing. It was simply a verification of what they suspected or had previously observed. There would be much more to learn.

Lunch concluded and the two parted company, at least for the time being. Jo began to walk back to the flat, her thoughts awash with the events of her meeting with her former lover. She pondered whether she was too quick in making the commitment. No, she thought. She had made the right choice. But, could she pull it off? More importantly, how would it affect her invaluable friendship with Fiona? Then there was the question as to whether the experience would change her. After all, she thought, look what happened to Peter. But, she decided, to dwell on all of this was counterproductive. She cleared her mind and focused on the next order of business, contacting Slattery and accepting the position with the Foundation while waiting for her next contact with the man she no longer knew.

Feeling overwhelmed from the events of the past couple of hours, Jo desperately needed a distraction. She was in no particular hurry to get back to Fiona's and have to deal with her dual identity. Some time to get her thoughts together and to reflect on the commitment she made was crucial. She had very little time to muster up a plan in order to carry forward the "deceit". "Deceit" was the word and no matter how unpleasant the thought, it was the reality with which she had to contend. The outcome of her afternoon with Peter brought her to think that he might know her better than she knew herself. After all, would he have approached her with the proposition if he wasn't reasonably sure that she would accept? The background on her probably included not only a security check but a psychological profile as well. Just how much did Peter and those he worked for, know about her and would they be able to manipulate her, at their whim? This was another complication in a day of complications and the day wasn't over.

Enough! She had to clear her mind, even if only for a little while. A bookstore sounded like a good idea. She walked down the narrow village streets weaving her way through the crowd of shoppers and others just out to enjoy the last of the pleasant weather. It wasn't more than a few minutes when she came upon a quaint and welcoming establishment, nestled inconspicuously between a couple of shops. It was one of those bookstores that catered to the academic community of the city. She entered the store and immediately her attention was called to a display featuring the great master, Leonardo da Vinci. As she walked over to that area of the bookstore, she thought back to Fiona's description of Slattery's library. How did she put it? It was something about the oddity of the combination of art, New Age and science. Maybe that wasn't odd, at all. Possibly the diversified interests were a reflection of whatever it is that he was working on. The library may not have been in conflict with his empirically oriented and pragmatic mind but, in fact, may have dovetailed with it. After all, da Vinci, himself, was a man who combined art, science and some things mysterious and history calls him a genius. Only time would tell if Slattery would rise to such lofty heights or be labeled another of history's dangerous eccentrics. The burden would be upon her to ferret out the truth.

She strolled over to the display and picked up what was one of those large, so-called, "coffee table" books which had on its cover a large reproduction of the famous da Vinci self portrait. She flipped through the book and as she scanned the pages she was reminded of the vast and sometimes bewildering knowledge of science which he possessed. He understood and drew the principles and mechanics of the helicopter centuries before conventional science developed such a craft. He had drawn a complete and accurate picture of a bicycle four hundred years before it was invented. She marveled at how Leonardo conceived of things mechanical even though they had no practical application in the world of his time. There are even those who postulate that he was the genius behind the Shroud of Turin and used knowledge and techniques in its creation which are still perplexing scientists, today. Jo paused to examine one of the pages more closely which had on it a grouping of a study on various shapes. Suddenly, she focused on one of those shapes which, to her eye, stood out above the rest. "I'll be damned", she blurted out, drawing some unwelcome stares. The illustration on which she fixed her attention was a depiction of the unusual logo which appeared below the name of the Foundation on the letterhead and the sign on the fence at the entrance to the compound.

[FORMATTER_INSERT IMAGE.JPG]

But why use some obscure sketch as a symbol for the Foundation? Could it have been some coincidence? Impossible. Was it simply whimsy? That was unlikely as Slattery was a man of science and not given to whimsy and the chances were good that the people behind the good Doctor were equally devoid of that characteristic. But, if the symbol had some direct meaning or represented something about the Foundation, it was not immediately apparent, at least not to her. The best course of action was to buy the book and give it a thorough review. Although she wasn't quite sure what she would be looking for, she had a gut feeling that, just by chance, she had stumbled onto something that would provide a clue to Slattery's activities.

The afternoon had sped by faster than Jo realized. It was 4:00 P.M. and a good, hot cup of tea was just the thing that she could use right now. She took a detour from her walk back to the flat and headed for the inviting little establishment that she spotted on the other side of the street. The day was still sunny and warm, so she pulled up a chair at one of the sidewalk tables to take advantage of what was left of the mild weather. A young waitress approached her with the usual,

"Good afternoon Miss, will there be anyone else joining you?"

"Good afternoon. No, no one."

"What might I get you?"

"I'll have a pot of Earl Gray. Do you have lemon cake with lemon curd sauce?"

"Yes, we do."

"Then, that's what I'll have."

"Thank you. I'll be right back with your tea and cake."

Tea and lemon cake with lemon sauce were her favorite things during times of anxiety when she was a student. "My god, I'm regressing to the point of eating comfort foods", was her reaction, laughing to herself. It was the first amusing thought that she had all day. But, she certainly needed comfort and if cake and tea were the only things available, they would have to do.

She sat there thinking of the events of the past few hours, occasionally taking a sip of the tea or a morsel of the cake, all the while paging through her recently purchased Da Vinci book, looking for something, anything which would provide, even indirectly, some insight into the Foundation. She had no factual or logical basis for her belief. It was only that, just a belief, but, she was certain that the symbol was not just a random choice, that it had a meaning, that there was more to be found in the text and that she would find it.

The tea room was located on a busy corner and the passing traffic momentarily distracted her, causing her to look up. There it was, the same Rover that had passed them when they were returning from the Foundation compound and, it seemed, with the same occupants. She was sitting at the outer edge of the sidewalk tables, close to the street and was no more than thirty feet from the vehicle. She couldn't help but stare, but, quickly caught herself and turned away. Being conspicuous or showing any unusual interest in these people or their activities might not be such a good idea. Anyway, they didn't seem to notice her. But, why should they? There was no reason to believe that they knew who she was or if they did, it was only that she was here at the request of Slattery. Certainly, they wouldn't know of her meeting with Peter, or care. According to Peter's explanation of his activities and procedures, there was not even any reason to believe that hey knew who Peter was or what he did. Given their past relationship, it would not be unusual for them to get together upon her arriving in England. So, why did they go by in front of the tea room at the precise time that she chose to be there? Well, Cambridge is a small area and as they say, everybody has to be someplace. Her rationale was unsatisfactory in warding off her suspicions. She remembered Peter's admonition about the possibility that anyone associated with Slattery might be watched. She finished up, paid the bill and began the walk back to the flat.

She wasn't sure whether or not Fiona would be home, but, chances were that she would. She was usually busy doing a great bit of her work out of the flat. Jo had to plan her approach to what would be her altered relationship with Fiona and she had to have it ready by the time she walked through the door. Peter had told her to change nothing, so, that's the way it would be. Rather than shutting Fiona out, she would collaborate with her on the Slattery matter, up to a point. It would make things run smoother and, hopefully, prevent questions from being raised.

After some minutes, she reached the apartment complex. Fiona had left the garage door open and the Jag was parked inside. Fiona was home. Jo took a deep breath, readied herself and entered the apartment.

"Fiona, are you here?"

"In the study."

Jo walked back to the alcove, off the living room, where Fiona was busy on her computer, intensely working on something or another, for her investment counseling business. It was a bright and cheery room, with potted plants liberally scattered about and French doors leading out to the balcony, letting in the light and warmth from the setting sun.

"Well, welcome home. Haven't we had a long afternoon with Peter", remarked Fiona in a jokingly suggestive manner, all the while maintaining her gaze at the computer screen in front of her.

"Very funny, but, the afternoon was purely platonic."

"Oh?", exclaimed Fiona, glancing up at Jo.

"I met with Peter at the wine bar across from King's and we had wine."

"Now who's being funny?"

"We ate, we drank, we talked."

"About any thing in particular?"

Jo paused to consider her answer.

"Not really. Just the usual stuff discussed by two people who had an incredibly hot relationship and haven't seen each other for ten years only to discover that the spark is as dead as it ever was."

"OK, OK, I get the message. Enough about Peter."

"Actually, the afternoon wasn't a total loss. After I met with Peter, I took a long walk and tried to sort out some questions as to this whole Slattery thing."

"Any revelations?"

"Nothing you could hang your hat on, but, I did come upon something which I think is pretty interesting."

"Such as?"

"This book."

Jo pulled the book out of a shopping bag, placed it on the desk where Fiona was working and turned to the page containing the illustration that was identical to the Foundation logo.

Fiona turned her attention away from the computer and to the book, flipping it back to the cover.

"Leonardo da Vinci?"

"No, no!", protested Jo. "Go back to the page I turned to and take a look", she insisted.

Fiona opened the book up and turned to the page that her friend had marked. Jo pointed to an illustration entitled, "Various studies in form".

"I'll be damned."

"That was exactly my reaction when I saw the sketch."

"But, what does it mean, that Slattery, or whoever, is a student of Renaissance art and chose this as a unique symbol for the Foundation?"

"No, I don't think so. Slattery is brilliant, but, in matters esthetic, he's a cold fish. No. there's something more to this, but, what, I don't know. I've a feeling that it goes back to that unusual set of books you saw in his office library that first day."

"And you're saying?"

"I don't know. What can you bring up on that computer of yours?"

"Just about everything having to do with investment. You know, stock quotes, real estate records, corporate records."

"That's it", interrupted Jo. "Pull up whatever services you use to see if we can get the description on the Foundation land and possibly information on ownership."

Even though Peter had told her of the difficulty in finding the underlying interests to the Foundation, it was her inclination to engage in some independent research as her way of sorting things out for herself and possibly, just possibly, shedding some light on this dark affair. It was also a good way to let Fiona participate without involving her in the larger picture.

Fiona skillfully went through the land and corporate records, as far back as she could go. It was as Peter said, a maze of organizations, most of them probably being shells, finally disappearing into the unfathomable world of the offshore company. Jo stared at the screen filled with names until something caught her eye.

"There". She put her finger on the screen over a company named "Vitruvian LTD."

"What about it?"

"You don't recognize the name?"

"Not offhand."

"You're not concentrating, but, I'll bet you'll recognize the picture."

Jo eagerly grabbed the book and rapidly went through the pages.

"There!", she exclaimed triumphantly, as she slapped the page on which appeared the famous da Vinci drawing of the nude male figure, arms outstretched and appearing in the middle of an intersecting square and circle. The legend below the illustration designated it as "Vitruvian Man". "It was discovered to be an algorithm. You know, a procedure for solving a problem. In this case it was for the purpose of squaring a circle or, to put it another way, to construct a circle and a square of equal area."

Fiona had been splitting her concentration between her work and Jo's explanation of the Da Vinci creation and was only partially listening.

"Are you getting all this."

"Yes, I'm listening."

"Just take a break from that damned computer a minute."

"OK, I'm all yours."

"According to the book, this algorithm is of particular significance."

"How so?"

"Because, it couldn't be figured out and turned into an equation without the aid of computer animations."

"You mean damned computer animations."

Jo gave a sigh of exasperation at Fiona's wisecrack.

"Just hear me out."

Jo continued her explanation.

"They gave up trying to figure this thing out with rulers and compasses, a long time ago. It couldn't be done in that fashion because ordinary methods restricted those trying to solve the problem to a finite number of steps. You had to have a means allowing a mathematical continuation into infinity, or, something which could project infinity in a virtual way."

Jo pointed to the instrument sitting in front of Fiona.

"A computer!"

"Interesting", observed Fiona. "You have a mathematical puzzle created in, let's see here", Fiona studied the legend below the illustration, "1492, which could only be solved with twentieth century technology."

"That's how it appears."

"It doesn't make sense."

"Yes it does, at least a type of sense. What you mean is that it doesn't make practical sense. But, you can get there if you want to carry a premise out to its logical conclusion. Creating something not of his time is consistent with what is known about da Vinci."

"True. But, creating a problem the solution of which is best illustrated by technology that comes along six to seven hundred years in the future? I don't know."

"Well, there it is."

"But, why?"

"The important question is, how."

"Got me. What are your thoughts?"

"I don't know, but I've been speculating. It's more than coincidence that the Foundation logo is a reproduction of a da Vinci sketch and a company in the chain of interests is named after a mathematical puzzle created by da Vinci."

Jo abruptly slammed the book shut and slumped back in the chair, head bowed and massaging her temples with her fingertips.

"I've had it. I'm going to take a long, hot bath."

"Take your time. I'll have a couple of martinis ready when you get through. I've got some stuff in the fridge, so, we'll just stay in tonight and have a late supper."

"Sounds great. See you in an hour."

With that, Jo retired to a much needed and much deserved tub of hot soapy water. She settled her energy drained body into the bath and the tensions of the day seemed to wash away. She closed her eyes and leaned her head back, almost asleep, but, not quite, in a state of being partly here and partly somewhere else. She heard the phone ring and Fiona answer. The voice of her friend seemed distant and she paid no attention to it. The comforting warmth of the water and the brief solitude were all that were important to her, at least for the next hour.

Some time passed, more time than she had realized and the water had turned from hot to tepid to cold. She got out of the bath, dried herself, slipped on a robe and made her way to the living room to see what Fiona was up to. It was already dark out and as she passed the kitchen she saw that the wall clock showed it to be 8:00 P.M. Some two hours had passed since she had gone in to take her one hour bath. She also realized that Fiona was nowhere to be found and found a note from Fiona, on the kitchen table.

"Jo,

Had to go out. Sorry. Be back late, so don't wait up.
I left dinner in the oven and a pitcher of
martinis in the fridge. See you in the morning."
Fiona"

There was no other explanation, but, she surmised, her friend's absence must have something to do with that telephone call that came in while she was in the tub. It was good to be alone and Fiona's absence took away some of the pressure, at least for the present. She was in a very relaxed and mellow mood. Thank god for hot baths and cold martinis, was her thought. She sat down at the kitchen table and picked at the food that Fiona had left for her. She wasn't very hungry, but, the martini was certainly just what the doctor ordered at this, the end of a most trying day.

She headed into the living room where she planned to lounge around for a while and catch up on the BBC News. She stretched out and switched on the TV. Nothing new. Same old stuff. Background noise. Talking heads, each trying to outdo the other to show their brilliance on whatever topic it was that they were jabbering about. Jo picked up the remote, pointed it at the TV and with deliberation, pressed the red button, ending the verbal chaos and blather that was intruding on her tranquility. She took a gulp of the martini and lay back on the sofa intending to relax a bit before going back to the book that had given forth some valuable nuggets of information. She hoped that, with a further and detailed reading of the text, more might be forthcoming. But, it was not to be, at least not tonight. It took only moments before she escaped into the sweet oblivion of sleep.

CHAPTER SIX

Jo opened her eyes, just barely. it was Wednesday morning and she was still on the sofa. She had never made it to bed last night and was suffering the consequences. She was feeling very creaky and stiff and doing her best to overcome a night of, what must have been, fitful sleep.

"Morning", chirped Fiona.

"Heavy date?, Jo queried, yawning and trying to throw off her grogginess.

"No, just some urgent business. You know, someone was in town and panic, panic, had to meet on some question that they felt had to be answered yesterday. Half of my business is holding someone's hand and reassuring them of something or another."

"Looks like you're off to the races, again."

"I'm afraid so. This time to Oxford. It's a carry over from last night. I'll be back late afternoon or early evening. What'll you be up to?"

"I'm going to take a walk to one of those auto rental places and pick up something on a monthly. By the way, can I borrow those binoculars you've got sitting on the bookshelf, over there?"

"Be my guest." Fiona gave her a stern look. "I don't know what you've got planned, but, be careful."

"Don't worry. I'm just going to observe some of the flora and fauna."

"Just make sure that some of the fauna don't observe you."

Fiona hurriedly stuffed some papers and files into her briefcase and started toward the door.

"See you later. By the way, I've left a pot of coffee on the countertop."

"Fiona, you're a lifesaver. Take care."

With that, Fiona closed the door behind her

Jo sat around for a while, planning her day. The hot, black coffee was ambrosia and was a much needed elixir to counter a fitful night on a sofa unsuitable for sleeping. The coffee was another example of how Fiona was always there when she needed her. It would be a great comfort if she could count on her dear friend to get her out of any trouble that she might encounter in this dangerous venture that she had undertaken. But, she knew that was not to be. She would, however, take Fiona's advice and tread carefully in carrying out the day's activities.

"Time to get a move on, Jo", she encouraged herself. Leaving the flat, she set out for the rental agency to pick up a car. The walk took her cross town to a place that she

had noticed on her way in, this past Friday. All she was interested in was basic transportation. Much to Fiona's disappointment, her love for fine automobiles never rubbed off on Jo, a frustration that sometimes led her to ask Jo, jokingly, if she was sure that she was really Italian. After arriving at the agency, it took her little time to pick out a red Mini. It wasn't much more than a small box with four wheels. But, it was enough for her purposes, although she was sure that Fiona would never approve. After taking care of the paperwork, other formalities and payment, she got behind the wheel and sped off, to what, she wasn't sure.

The little car was actually quite quick and responsive and she was very self satisfied with her selection. She traveled the now familiar route which took her past the entrance road to the compound and took a glance down the road as she passed it by and continued on. Her self appointed task was to find another path that would take her somewhere near the perimeter of the compound, provide some cover and allow her a view of the grounds. Perhaps, she would see something that she was and would be prevented from seeing with Slattery hovering over her.

As she drove, she continued checking her rear view mirror, often, to see if she was being followed. It didn't seem that she was, at least not by the black Rover. Although she was feeling some anxiety, there was also a sense of exhilaration about the whole thing. Yes, in a real sense, she was enjoying herself in a way that she had never known and she didn't understand her new emotions. Could it be, as she thought back to her meeting at the wine bar, that

Peter picked her for this because he really did know her better than she knew herself?

Jo continued driving, searching for some road or path that would give her the desired vantage point. It was frustrating. She had gone off road a couple of times onto paths barely wide enough to accommodate, even, her small car. She could no longer deal with the spine-jarring potholes, scraping the bottom of the car, hoping that she didn't rip out the oil pan or the gas tank and the low branches of the trees and the hedges beating the paint job to death. She would have to find an alternative before she turned her rental into a pile of junk.

The surrounding topography had some hilly and high points. Rather than getting next to the compound, it seemed that she could find a vantage point looking down at the compound. It might be more distant, but, that's what binoculars were for. She checked the rear view mirror again. Nothing there. "So far, so good", she said to herself. Maybe she was getting too edgy. But, then again, it could be that it wasn't a mild case of paranoia. Instead, it was a logic driven awareness and survival instincts manifesting themselves.

Jo drove to an area that was halfway up a hill and about a quarter mile from the rear boundary of the compound. She pulled the car off the road, behind some bushes which would give her a measure of cover although, under the circumstances, she was unhappy with herself at the choice of red as the color for the car. She knew that she wouldn't have much time as she was sure that someone would be coming up or down the road and Fiona's admonition kept running through her mind. She would do the best she could and then get the hell out of there. She took the binoculars, put the lenses to her eyes and leaned on the roof of the car, with her elbows, in order to steady her view. After some adjustment, she got a clear and focused view of the compound and its surroundings. This location gave her a different perspective of the grounds. Although she couldn't see the front entrance of the wooden building, the concrete building was angled in such a way so as to allow her to view its front entrance. She was also able to get a good perspective as to the brick buildings that raised her interest during her initial visit to the Foundation. Again, there was no sign of outside activity, which disappointed her. She figured that the activities must be run according to a strict regimen and that she simply hit it at the wrong time, for the second time. The more likely answer was that those at the compound were simply kept out of sight. But, why? And aside from the technicians, Slattery and Jack, who else worked or resided at the compound?

As she panned around, her attention was caught by Slattery and Jack standing at the front entrance to enigmatic concrete building. She couldn't hear them and cursed herself for not being able to read lips. It did appear that Slattery was displeased with his stalwart assistant and from the gestures he was making and his pointing to the door, it seemed that he was reprimanding Jack for not having properly secured it. This was something that she would mentally catalogue for possible use at a later date. Perhaps, Jack, in spite of his ominous and threatening bearing, was actually a weak link in the security of the compound and some oversight or carelessness, on his part, might give her an opportunity, in the future.

She trained her binoculars on the brick buildings. There was some movement. A door of one of the buildings partially opened. Her gaze intensified and the wait to see who emerged, although only seconds passed, the wait was excruciating. She watched, but, could see no one, only a hand holding on to the inside knob as they slowly pushed the door open. Suddenly, her attention was drawn to the roar of an engine, somewhat distant, but, approaching rapidly, from down the hill. She continued to peer through the binoculars, dividing her attention between what she was looking at and the approaching sound, all the while attempting to calculate how much time she had before she had to break off her observation of the compound. She couldn't see who or what was approaching her as the road curved around from the point where she had positioned herself.

"Damn it! Come on. Come on out. Let me see who you are", she anxiously implored of the mysterious person attached to the hand holding the door knob. She was frustrated at both the person behind the door for taking so long to come out and the motorist for interrupting her at this critical moment. Time was up! She tossed the binoculars onto the front seat, got into the car and tried not to look out of place, if that was possible. She pulled out a roadmap and opened it up, laying it across the steering wheel. The lost tourist gambit was as good as any.

She sat and waited, listening to what now seemed to be a motorcycle approaching from the rear. The engine revved down as it got closer, but, she kept her attention on the map spread out before her. The cycle stopped next to the car and she looked up. The cycle was bright yellow and one of those uncomfortable looking racing types that Fiona referred to as a "Crotch Rocket". The rider was dressed in a black windbreaker, blue jeans and a black crash helmet, one of those with a face visor that covers everything. She was relieved. Her first thought was that it might be Jack, the omnipresent guard of the Foundation, bearing down on her. But, the clothes were much too casual. Jack would probably be outfitted in much more severe regalia; boots, black leathers, all that. The rider removed his helmet and Jo found herself looking at a young man. She sized him up to be in his early to mid twenties, about six feet tall with light brown hair, slightly long and very handsome, bordering on pretty, if it were not for a certain indefinable ruggedness in his face that enhanced the masculine quality. It was certainly a pleasant surprise as she caught herself giving him the once over.

"May I be of assistance, Miss?"

"No, I'm fine. Just getting the lay of the land."

"American?"

"Yes, as a matter of fact I am."

"New York?"

"You are a perceptive young man. Where did you come by your knowledge of American accents?"

"I have a certain aptitude for accents and many other things."

"Yes", Jo paused and contemplated the young man before her, "I'll bet you do."

"Well, if you're alright, I'll be on my way."

"He turned the engine on, revved it a couple of times and turned to Jo, giving her a slight wave.

"Ciao."

She smiled and nodded.

He roared off, turning back, just briefly, to look at her, before he accelerated out, rounded the uphill curve and disappeared.

Jo sat there for a moment, reflecting on the encounter. She decided that she had done enough for the day, folded the map, which was still perched on the steering wheel and started back to Cambridge. She took the longer route, continuing up the hill, rather than back down, on the chance that she might spot the young man on the motorcycle. She had no plan should she see him, but, he instilled a curiosity in her. No luck. He was long gone.

Jo arrived back at the flat and got down to the business that was the reason for her coming to Cambridge in the first place. She knew that she had better be prepared to accomplish the tasks that would be required of her at the Foundation or her tenure would be a short one and Peter's master plan would be in the toilet. She pulled out her files and spent the rest of the afternoon going over her own research notes that she had brought along on the trip. It was a ponderous chore. The cloak and dagger stuff was much more stimulating, But, what had to be done, had to be done.

Jo lost track of time and when she looked at her watch it was 6:45 in the evening. The afternoon had come and gone when she heard a key in the door. Fiona was back.

"Greetings. How'd the Oxford trip go?"

"Good. But, I'm bushed. Do me a favor and pour me a scotch, neat, while I freshen up and change."

Jo poured a couple of scotches, relaxed in the living room and waited for Fiona to come out.

After a few minutes, her friend appeared.

"That feels much better. Let me have that scotch."

Fiona took the glass and raised it.

"Cheers."

"Cin cin."

"That is good", remarked Fiona sipping her drink as she reached for the black box, which was her constant companion and removed a cigarette. She lit up a John Player, took a deep drag and tilted her head back as she exhaled, watching the smoke billow upward. "So tell me about your little excursion out to the country."

"I rented a Mini and took a two hour drive, just to clear the cobwebs. I also took a detour over to an area overlooking the Foundation to see what I could see."

"Your Mini's the red thing I saw parked in the extra space, downstairs?"

"That's the one."

"You really are going to have to do something about your taste in cars."

"Please, don't start."

"By the way, make good use of the binoculars, did you?"

"I just wanted to get a good look at the compound grounds. I don' think Slattery's prepared to give me a guided tour."

"So, what'd you see?"

"Well, the land extends back for a pretty good distance beyond the lab buildings. Just some pasture and a few horses and cows grazing. That's about it."

Jo wanted to move the subject away from the Foundation itself, to avoid discussing anything further of her observations and motivations, with Fiona.

"I did cross paths with a young man while I was parked at the side of the road taking a look at the compound. He thought I was a damsel in distress and offered me some help."

"Did he see the binoculars?"

"No. By the time he got to me, I was sitting in the car, looking at a map and playing lost tourist. He was charming, actually, intriguing. Very bright. He pegged me for a New Yorker, right off the bat."

"Any other details?"

"Other than the fact that he was an extraordinarily good looking guy, nothing comes to mind. I suppose he was just out for a ride. He came out of nowhere, stopped and continued on to nowhere. He wasn't British or, at least, didn't have an English accent."

"Oh?"

"He had a trace of some sort of accent, but, I couldn't place it."

"I'd be a lot more careful in the future. You never know. I'm assuming that your little expedition is an indicator that you're going to give a 'yes' to Slattery's offer."

"Yeah."

"When are you going to let him know?"

"At the end of the week."

"You're going to wait till the deadline?"

"I think so. You know, let him sweat a bit."

"You think he'll be sweating it out waiting for your answer?"

"I have a feeling he will."

"You are a cruel one, you are", remarked Fiona, jokingly, looking at Jo out of the corner of her eye and shaking her head in mock disapproval.

"I know", Jo said, laughingly. "But, sometimes it can be such fun."

"By the way, have you given any more thought to the stuff in your da Vinci book?"

"No, not really. I've been trying to do some preparation so I'll be ready to start at the Foundation and that's coming up fast, too fast."

"And you never thought about scrapping it?"

"It crossed my mind, early on."

"Well. you might as well see where it goes."

"That's how I'm thinking", avoiding any indication that her association with the Foundation had gone beyond free choice and that she had passed the point of no return, not only because of her promise to Peter, but, also as a result of the depth of her own personal commitment.

"Do you know if Dr. Miller is still with the college?" queried Jo.

"Cyril Miller?"

"Yeah."

"He's still there. As a matter of fact, he was one of Slattery's most outspoken critics and was the driving force that got him removed from the faculty. There's a lot of bad blood between them. Are you thinking of contacting him?"

"I'm giving it serious consideration. I'd like to get all the background I can on Slattery. It'll just make me more comfortable with the whole situation."

"Well, I don't know how much of a firestorm you'll run into, but, I would expect that Miller will be surprised that you're hooking up with Slattery and he won't be very happy about that."

"I think I can get past that. We got along very well in the old days. I hope he's in town."

"I would think so. He should be getting ready to start the new session."

"It'll be interesting to see what he has to say."

"I don't think he'll know mush about what's going on at the Foundation, right now, but, he should have some pretty good inside information as to what got Slattery into so much hot water which cost him his position at the college."

"I hope so."

"Oh, don't worry. He does."

"How can you be so sure?"

"Because, Slattery tried to pull Miller with him, but, Miller would have none of it. When he got a clue as to what Slattery was up to, it all hit the fan. Once Slattery left, the college washed its hands of the whole thing and kept a very tight lid on it."

"If it was so bad, how come somebody didn't blow the whistle?"

"You know better than that. Old and staid institutions don't gain power, longevity and wealth by being activists and striking out on controversial and righteous crusades. When Slattery was gone, so was the problem, as far as the college was concerned. You have at least one advantage. Martin is still the day porter and I'm sure he'll do all he can for you."

"That is good news. He's a great guy and I'll be glad to see him again. He was such a character. He had this vision of what New York was like and always thought of me as some wayward kid from the city. He took me under his wing and treated me like a third daughter. It's something positive to look forward to. We'll have to see how it goes tomorrow."

CHAPTER SEVEN

The digital clock on the nightstand read Thursday", in bold, green letters. But, Jo didn't need a clock to tell her that. The inexorable clock of unstoppable time, which waits for no man, or woman, was indeed ticking and it was the day before she would have to call Slattery and give him an answer, committing herself to start work at the Foundation. There was no time to waste. She washed up, dressed hurriedly and rushed past Fiona who was already up and reading the paper.

"I'm heading over to the college to try and get in to see Miller. I'll catch some coffee on the way."

"Good luck!"

Jo dashed out, slamming the door behind her, in her haste. She would walk rather than drive as it would take less time, the parking being as bad as it was in and about Cambridge. Besides, the morning air was invigorating and gave her a chance to clear out the cobwebs.

After a brisk, ten minute stroll, she came upon the archway at the entrance of the college. The large, heavy, timber double gate had been opened this day as it had every day for hundreds of years, to accommodate the daily influx of people consisting of the last of the tourists as well as some of the early arrival students anticipating the new session.

She went through the entrance, turned into a side hallway and climbed a couple of steps which took her to the doorway of the porter's lodge. She peeked in without actually entering. It was as she remembered it. Why shouldn't it be? Except for some electric lights it was, in all probability, unchanged since the late eighteen hundreds. It was old, but, light and cheery and had the thick plastered walls, woodwork and planked floors which gave testament to its age. The office was almost completely filled up with the large dark wood desk at its center which was piled high, as she remembered it always was, with papers files and records. The traditional black cap and jacket of a porter's uniform was hanging from a hat rack off in the corner of the room. The room was identifiable as existing in the twenty first century only by virtue of the presence of a computer perched on a shelf behind the desk.

Although the man occupying the chair had his back to her, she recognized him as her old friend Martin by the full head of reddish-blond hair, which was always a distinguishing feature and as best she could observe, it had not thinned out as a result of passing time. She glanced at a small group of photographs, propped up on the side of the desk which was closest to the wall and recognized Martin's wife, Margaret and the two lovely young ladies, obviously the daughters that, once upon a time, she would babysit on the rare occasions that Marin would take an evening out with his better half.

She found him in the familiar position of being stooped over, digging through a file cabinet drawer, looking for some document or another, probably to assist an incoming student with the preparation and arrangements for their room and board. Jo stood at the door for a moment and finally addressed the porter who was so completely absorbed in his task.

"Martin?" she said, in a quiet and slightly questioning tone.

The man who had, but a moment ago, been totally focused on the task at hand suddenly stopped what he was doing and straightened up in his chair, without immediately turning around.

"Oh my, oh my, could it be?"

"Yes it could", Jo responded to the man she had not seen in ten years and was one of the people that she most missed from her days at University.

Martin finally turned his chair around to face Jo and revealed the smiling face and jovial personality that she had remembered. It was a face which made him look younger than his years. Martin was a good man who, every once in a while, would break a minor rule, or two, in order to accommodate a student and there were more than a few times, during her years at the college, when she was the recipient of such favors. He always had a soft spot for her and now and then he was a shoulder to cry on during those days when things got toughest. He enjoyed the fact that she was such a stereotypical New Yorker, accent and all, which made her stand out from the other students. He had always been impressed by her and their discussions of Manhattan and vowed that one day he would take his family to visit her city.

"My goodness, look at you", beamed Martin as he rose from his chair and made his way around the desk to greet her.

"Please, please, sit down." he pulled up a chair and guided her by the arm to her seat, always maintaining the proper reserve expected of one occupying his position.

"This is a wonderful surprise. When did you get in?"

"The end of last week."

"If you need, I'd be delighted to make arrangements here at the college, for a room during your stay."

"Thanks, but I'm staying with Fiona Clark."

"Ah, yes. Then two of you were always inseparable. Oh, forgive me. I'm getting chatty and I haven't even offered you any refreshment. There's a fresh pot of tea. Would you care for a cup?"

"That sounds good, thanks."

Martin went over to where he kept a small burner, just for the purpose of making his tea which he, unlike Fiona, simply could not do without. He busied himself with the preparation while continuing his conversation with Jo, remembering her student days. After a short while of reminiscing, they brought the conversation to the present.

"You know, me and the family finally made it to New York."

"I'm glad. I hope it lived up to your expectations."

"That it did."

"When did you go?"

"In the summer of two thousand. So, we were fortunate to be able to see the World Trade Center. Terrible business, that attack. Watched the whole bloody thing on the telly."

"Yes, it was a terrible thing", Jo responded, reflectively.

Martin poured two cups of tea, handing one to Jo. She took a sip, settled back in the chair and closed her eyes as if remembering herself in this very place, ten years ago.

"Ah, just like old times. Isn't it Martin?"

"Yes, yes. In some ways it is very much like old times with you in the office and sharing a morning pot of tea. And if my memory serves me correctly, some crisis or another usually accompanied our little meetings." Martin looked at her with a knowing grin.

Jo, feeling a bit self-conscious, smiled back, sheepishly.

"Never could get anything past you, Martin. Actually, it's more of a favor than a crisis."

"Well, whatever it is, I'm here to give you a hand."

"I know and I've always been thankful for that."

Jo thought for a moment as to how she wanted to present her situation to Martin. She always had to make sure that she didn't inadvertently say too much and holding back information from Martin or telling half truths was almost as hard with him as it was with Fiona.

"I've got to be frank with you Martin, I'm in Cambridge at the invitation of Ian Slattery to join him at the Foundation and assist him in his research."

Martin interrupted Jo's explanation, an uncharacteristically stern look on his face.

"And this is something you've considered carefully?"

"Yes."

"And something you'd not reconsider?"

"No."

"This doesn't sound like something I can help you with. What in the world could I possibly do?"

"I would like to see Dr. Miller."

"Dr. Cyril Miller?"

"Yes."

Martin leaned back in his chair. He was obviously troubled by Jo's request in light of the fact that she was to be in association with Ian Slattery.

"May I assume that you wouldn't be asking me to arrange this unless you knew of the, shall we say situation, that exists between Dr. Miller and Dr. Slattery?"

"Fiona gave me some details."

"Then we'll keep it between you and me and I'll call up to Dr. Miller and tell him that you've come here just to say hello. At least you'll get your foot in the door. I'll leave it to you to break the news to him as to your real reason for being here. I can't guarantee what his reaction will be. But, at least it will probably be one of great annoyance. You can be assured of that."

Martin picked up the phone, dialed a few numbers and waited for a moment.

"Dr. Miller? This is Martin at the porter's lodge. Thank you and good morning to you to, sir. I have a young lady, or should I say a young American female geneticist who has just arrived in Cambridge and would like to duck in and say hello."

"Yes Doctor. Yes it is. It was a pleasant surprise for me also. I'll send her up directly."

He hung up the receiver and turned back to Jo. "It's all set."

"Thanks Martin. You're a dear."

"I would suggest you save the thanks pending Dr Miller's reaction. Fortunately, it sounds like you've caught him in one of his better moods."

"Is he in the same residence?"

"Yes, indeed. Past the court, through the archway, second floor to the right."

"Got it and don't worry. If it comes up, I'll make sure that he doesn't think that you know why I'm really here."

Well, good luck."

Jo left the porter's lodge and walked the familiar route, arriving at Miller's rooms. The door was slightly ajar. She took a deep breath and gave a gentle knock.

"Come in", beckoned the deep and robust voice from inside the residence.

Jo pushed the door the rest of the way open and cautiously walked in.

"Leave it partially open. It improves the ventilation in this exceptionally warm weather."

Miller was in the process of lighting up his ever present and usually foul smelling pipe that she remembered so well. He was about the same age as Slattery, but, somewhat shorter. He seemed hardly to have aged over the last decade and still sported a military haircut with a short beard and moustache both of which were now salt and pepper giving some evidence to the fact that appreciable time had passed since she last saw him. He was still very fit, actually trained and was given to wearing jeans and golf shirts which revealed his trim and muscular physique.

"You don't mind the pipe do you?"

"Not at all.." Actually she did. But, some diplomacy was called for.

Miller took a couple of puffs and sent out a plume of thick, acrid tobacco smoke which hung heavy in the air.

Jo surveyed Miller's quarters and they were just as same as ten years ago. The walls were covered with book shelves with some pieces of furniture being added seemingly as an afterthought, purely out of necessity.

"Please, sit down."

"Thank you, Doctor. Let me start off by telling you why I'm here so I don't waste your time. I'm afraid I was less than candid with Martin. But, I felt that it was imperative that I see you."

"Don't fret about it, Joanna. I know why you're here."

At that moment a feeling of both surprise and relief, tinged with a bit of embarrassment, came over her. At least everything was in the open and Miller would be receptive to her inquiries even though he might be staunchly against what she was doing. The meeting would be far better than she could have expected.

"News travels fast", she commented.

"It does in a place such as this. No doubt the information was leaked by Slattery for his own reasons."

"I haven't formalized anything yet, but, I do intend to make a commitment to Dr. Slattery, even if it's only for a short duration."

"I don't know what Slattery has told you or what he promised you, but, it's my opinion that he'll do nothing to enhance your career and will, in all likelihood, damage it. He's become a pariah. The path he chose, some years ago, caused him to be ostracized by the University, not to mention many of those in the scientific community, some of them having been colleagues. This is despite the fact that he has succeeded in acquiring standing and notoriety in the international community because of his ties, how he holds himself out and the supposed humanitarian work that the Foundation does, ostensibly for the betterment of mankind. It's all rubbish, absolute rubbish."

Miller was composed, but, she could sense his agitation at her decision to associate herself with Slattery. He wasn't irritated at her as much as he was concerned for her.

"I was told of the situation with Slattery after I arrived in Cambridge. Fiona gave me some information, but, she didn't know that much."

"I can't say for certain what Slattery is up to, but, I will tell you what I know."

Miller began to relate, to Jo, Slattery's decline at Cambridge and his joining up with a clandestine international consortium which established the Serpentine Foundation and put him in charge of it.

"Make no mistake about it, Slattery was and is a brilliant scientist, but, some years ago he began to suffer an overabundance of dissatisfaction with his lot."

"In what way?" asked Jo.

"He had an outstanding reputation and position with the University, but, as he progressed in years and began to look back, as we all do, he discovered that this wasn't enough. He became driven by an unhealthy and overwhelming desire, no, an overwhelming and unhealthy obsession to elevate himself to a level so that the name, Dr. Ian Slattery would be mentioned in the same breath with Watson and Crick."

"Isn't that what we all aspire to?"

"Not all, but, some. And when that becomes the focus of one's personal and professional existence, it is crucial as to what road we travel to attain the outcome."

"And you're saying that Dr. Slattery took the wrong road?"

"I can't make that statement with a certainty, but, towards the end of his tenure, he became extremely unorthodox in his viewpoints to the extent that it began to cripple him in both the scientific and academic communities.

"Fiona did mention that Dr. Slattery had been referred to, jokingly, as the 'mad doctor'."

"Well, if not mad, then, surely, alarmingly eccentric."

"I have to say, that in my meeting and conversation with him, this past Monday, he was exuberant, but, not more than that."

"In all probability, it is his attempt to put you at ease and draw you in. I assume, from reading some of what you've recently published, that he has you over here because of your work in the area of what is loosely designated as genetic memory."

"That's what we discussed. I'm sure you've concluded my work's at a very primitive stage."

"It's likely that whatever he represented to you is a front and that he has something else in store when he gains confidence in your loyalty by convincing you, to his satisfaction, that you are willing to participate in his delusions of grandeur, whatever those might be. Make no mistake about it, he has you here because you are able to serve his primary purpose and that of the Foundation. What that may be is unclear. One thing is for certain, it isn't to feed the hungry of the world."

Jo sat there in silence, momentarily contemplating what Miller was relating and piecing it together with what she was told in her conversation with Peter. She also wanted to learn as much as possible, as to the nature of the rift between Miller and Slattery. There was no easy way to approach that subject. She would simply have to take the initiative and bring it up.

"It's not my intention to impose, Doctor, but I understand that you and Doctor Slattery had a personal confrontation and split over this matter."

"It's quite right and appropriate that you ask. You should be armed with as many of the facts as possible, in anticipation of your pending association."

The meeting with Miller was going much better than Jo could have anticipated and she was relieved at his response of cooperation as to her inquiry. She listened, with anticipation, as he continued.

"A few years ago, something turned Slattery's attention to what we're calling, for want of a better term, genetic memory. But, it wasn't within the framework of the scientific and benign research in which you're involved. No, it was and is something entirely different. Slattery was contacted by an international consortium and attended a couple of clandestine meetings in London."

"Why do you think Dr. Slattery was chosen?"

"I believe that people such as those in the consortium, or syndicate, or whatever it may be, have an instinct for people such as Slattery, like the spider which instinctively spins its web to catch the hapless fly. Slattery was a man in a state of professional dissatisfaction. He was afraid, in a way, that his life, in spite of all the work he'd done, would end in failure or, at least, failure as he perceived it. The Doctor, I'm afraid, given his state of mind, at the time,

CHAPTER EIGHT

Friday had arrived. It would be a busy day and there would be no time to waste. Jo arose early and expected to see the familiar sight of Fiona busying herself in the kitchen. But, as she walked down the hall from the bedroom, she didn't hear any activity in the flat. Fiona had not returned. She stopped and glanced at the ashtray that contained the burned down John Player. For that moment, it absorbed her attention, becoming the focus of her thoughts and she began to consider its ominous implications. Fiona had not called. She checked the answering machine, just to make sure. The machine counter was at "0". She tried Fiona's cell number, again. But, again the response was the same. There was no response. She considered leaving a message, letting her friend know that she would be staying at the college for the weekend, but, thought the better of it. She was uncomfortable and suspicious with Fiona's unexplained absence in light of the events of the week.

Although it was unlikely that Fiona's present absence was related to her activities, Jo could not help but think that such an occurrence might take place in the future resulting from their friendship and association. She would go to the college, do what she had to do and wait until she came back to the flat, at the end of the weekend to see if Fiona had returned. She didn't like the thought of not leaving a note which, knowing Fiona, would lead her to concern, but that's the way it would have to be.

She went to the closet, pulled out a piece of luggage and packed what she would need for the weekend and for tonight's dinner. She started for the door and stopped, abruptly. "Might as well get the acceptance call to Slattery over with", she thought to herself. She dialed up the number, given to her by the Dr., and was greeted by a recorded message. It was the flat, impersonal and unwelcoming voice of Jack. Just as well. She wouldn't have to deal with Slattery and complicate her morning. Jack's message ended with the familiar beep.

"Good morning Dr. Slattery, this is Dr. Russo. It's Friday at 8:30 AM and I'm calling to let you know that I accept your offer to work at the Foundation. I'll be there Monday, to start, under the terms that we previously discussed. See you then."

" Got that off my back", she mumbled to herself, as she hung up the phone.

She picked up her suitcase and stopped at the door, looking back at the empty flat, pensively. She turned around, left and hurried down to the red Mini, parked on the street, below. She arrived at the college and in minutes, found a parking space, grabbed her overnight bag and walked to the porter's lodge to say hello to Martin for the keys to the residence. He was extremely busy with the crush of incoming students and could only offer a perfunctory greeting. She took the keys and made her way across the court to the oldest wing of the college and up the narrow staircase which led to a cramped, second floor landing. She entered the residence and saw that Martin had outdone himself, once again. She loved the rooms in the old court. There was always an aura of majesty about the place when one considered how many had passed through these rooms over hundreds of years. Even the ever present mustiness of age lent to the texture and ambiance of the place. There was no phone, TV, cable or otherwise, or radio and certainly no air conditioning, which was scarce anywhere in the city. Any inconvenience, however, was more than offset by the sense of history which washed over anyone who was fortunate enough to find themselves in a place such as this. The sitting room was large and spacious and comfortably furnished. It had a fireplace which no longer used wood as a fuel, but, had been replaced, decades ago, with a gas burner, a device fondly remembered, by her own past experience, to have been totally inefficient in heating anything during the cold months. Over the mantle, crossed oars, emblazoned with the coat of arms of the College and University, were proudly placed indicating that this was the residence of the captain of the rowing team, an upper classman who had not yet arrived for the fall session. The bed chamber, which housed one single bed that looked more like a large cot was off the sitting room and was tiny by American standards. In addition to the bed, there was a small chest of drawers and a very old rickety armoire that looked like it had been put there by the original occupant. The small bedroom window was heavily barred as were all the windows at the college, which faced the street. Once locked up for the night, the college was a veritable fortress where no one could get in and once in, could not leave, without the night porter, the keeper of the keys, unlocking the small entry door within the massive wooden gates. Just below the bedroom window was a gate and narrow walkway and on the other side of the walkway there was one of those very old cemeteries that she would ponder during her student days. They were, as this one was, usually in some out of the way corner, well kept but with simple headstones bearing the date of death, made faint with time, showing the grave to be hundreds of years old, with the names of the souls lying beneath, wiped away by the elements, now unknown and forgotten. *Is this the final legacy of us all, she thought, or, is there something more; a common thread, undiscovered, which links us all? Is this what was driving Slattery?*

Jo unpacked. She wasn't particularly hungry, but, went down to the dining hall to get something to fortify her for the task ahead. The hall was relatively empty. That would change in a week or so when the session was in full swing. As she went in, there was a table to the right on which stood one of those large electric coffee urns and a huge, ancient, pea green toaster which looked like the one that sat in the same place when she was a student and, in all likelihood, was. She got herself some coffee and toast and sat down at one of the long tables that stretched from the entrance of the hall almost all the way to the other end stopping just short of the area in which was located High Table. The dining hall had always reminded her of a church with its high, arched ceiling, tall cathedral windows, carved wood ornamentation and oil paintings of historical individuals, some associated with the University. High Table sat on a raised platform at the back of the hall. If the hall, itself, reminded one of a church, then High Table was its altar and, in fact, was treated as such. It was a hallowed area, prohibited to most except for the fellows and dons, the high priests of the University community. She had always held a reverence for the traditions of Cambridge and was honored and gratified for the opportunity, provided by Miller, to attend tonight's dinner.

But, time was flying by and she had to make the most of her two days at the college. She finished up and left the dining hall to make her way to the storage closet to collect the boxes that Miller had told her about. Just as Miller described, there were three innocuous looking, cardboard, file storage boxes, marked, "Dr. Ian Slattery", sitting at the far right-hand corner of the closet. She stacked the boxes, one on top of the other and found that she could carry them back to her residence without any help. She brought them back to her rooms and settled in to go through the contents, hoping that she had not been overly optimistic about what their contents might give up in the way of insight into Slattery.

She began rummaging through the first box and found the usual things which one might leave behind, a couple of ashtrays, a pen set and various other articles of junk. There was, however, an old day planner which Jo set aside for inspection. The second box contained nothing of importance. But, the third box, which was the heaviest, contained some notebooks and a leather bound journal, which was of particular interest. Perhaps this was the treasure trove she was looking for and documents thought of by Slattery to be unimportant, at the time, might now give those, attempting to uncover his secrets, a window or, at least, open that window a crack to provide some revelations. It was times like this that made her wish that she hadn't given up smoking.

She decided to start her research with a review of the day planner. Luck was with her. It was Slattery's day planner for the last year before he left the college and contained dates relevant to the events that led up to that point. A glance at the first page in the book showed that Slattery was a meticulous record keeper, so, it was fair to assume that whatever he did and whenever and wherever he did it would appear as an entry in the day planner. As she thumbed through the pages, she reflected how many times such complete and thorough memoranda, concerning one's activities worked against those keeping such records and why they never seemed to learn.

The log was interesting, but, commonplace. There was much of Slattery's ordinary professional activities recorded and some odd bits, here and there, such as the meetings in London, although no particular site was designated nor names of those with whom he met. She was able to get through the pages quickly and only stopped for a second look towards the end where he had penned in some places and times relating to his vacation in France. But, it was incomplete. Miller had told her that Slattery had taken a one month vacation. According to the planner, the month was July, but, only the first twenty six days of the month were accounted for. Could this have been simple carelessness or neglect? Unlikely as such omissions occurred nowhere else..

She was distracted from her task by a knock at the door. She went over and opened it to find a very young man, about eighteen or nineteen, standing outside, on the landing.

"May I help you?", Jo inquired.

The young man stood there speechless, his eyes fixed on the woman standing before him. She was dressed in sandals, tight jeans, with that worn look, hugging her tall, lean modelish figure, one of those revealing tank tops, no makeup covering her slightly olive skin, revealing her natural and sensuous beauty, all topped by a thick tousled mane of dark brown hair. It was simply too much for such a young man to take in, all at one time, and keep his wits about him.

"May I help you?", Jo repeated, attempting to elicit a response.

"Are you Dr. Russo, Dr. Joanna Russo?", the young man haltingly queried as if unsure that he was at the right place.

"Yes, I am."

"Martin sent me up to tell you that Dr. Miller has invited you for cocktails at the Fellow's private lounge at 7:00 o'clock, tonight."

"Tell Martin, thanks for the message and that I'll be there."

Jo took a step back and began to close the door, but, noticed that the young man continued to stare as he started walking backwards on the landing.

"I suggest that you turn around before you take a nasty tumble down the stairs.", she warned him, giving him a smile.

He snapped out of his trance and turned around, just in time, disappearing down the staircase. Jo closed the door behind her, intending to back to her research, shaking her head and quietly chuckling to herself, thinking of the flustered young messenger.

She retrieved the journal that had previously caught her eye and, in that it bore the earliest date of the rest of the materials in the remaining box consisting of a series of notebooks, would be the logical starting point. It was about eight by ten inches in dimension, dark brown leather, in good condition, with one of those snap closures and about two inches thick. It was filled with narrowly lined pages, filled in with writing, neat and precise. If she wanted to do a thorough job, it would take her through the rest of the morning and the afternoon to cover it completely.

Jo went over to one of the large, old easy chairs which was positioned with its back to the window with the warm sunlight streaming in, a perfect place to spend the morning and do what she had to do. She sat there, curled up on the chair, turning page after page, always anticipating that while one page would tell her nothing of importance, the next one would say something, anything. The writings tended to be philosophical in nature as to Slattery's reflections of science, in general and genetics, in particular. The journal was dated the year previous to Slattery leaving the college and seemed to be a prelude to his disenchantment with his position there and his anticipated future which, according to Miller, he saw as nothing more than a dead end.

Jo was entirely absorbed in her task and before she realized it, the morning had passed and her watch told her that it was noon. She lifted her eyes from the pages, for the first time in three fruitless hours, yawned and decided that it was time for a break. She went over to the sink, splashed some cold water on her face and looked at her reflection in the mirror realizing that some different clothing was in order. A faded, blue work shirt would do nicely. There was no sense in upsetting any more of the young male population of Cambridge, or, the old male population, for that matter. There would be no leisurely pub lunch today. There was no time and, anyway, she was too wound up to eat. An espresso sounded good. She would find the first place that sold espresso, get herself a double and bring it back to drink while she continued her research.

As she passed the fireplace, on her way out, she noticed a small wooden frame hanging under the crossed oars and which had escaped her attention in her distraction with other things. It contained something printed which looked like it had been cut out of a book. She stopped to read it.

> "*Show wisdom. Strain clear the wine; and since life is brief, cut short far reaching hopes! Even while we speak, envious Time has sped. Reap the harvest of today, putting as little trust as may be in the morrow.*"
> (Horace)

She exited the college and walked down the street. The words echoed through her mind. They comprised a thought which she found unique to be posted in the dorm room of a university student, a person one would have thought to be too caught up in their ambition to achieve along with dealing with the traditional diversions of college life to be reflecting on the profundity of time and life. The quotation contained in the inconspicuous wooden frame spoke of a person, occupying those rooms, as possessing extraordinary perception. The words unexpectedly impacted her as she thought of how her life had been turned upside down in just the space of one week and how her focus on long range professional goals had been transformed into an existence where she couldn't be sure, to any reasonable extent, what the next hour, much less the next day, would bring.

After exiting the college gates and walking a couple of blocks down the street she came upon a cafe, located above a market. "ESPRESSO SERVED", indicated the welcoming words of the sign. Jo took the stairs to the second level and entered the friendly, little, crowded cafe. She noticed the welcome sight of an espresso machine just outside the small kitchen. The girl behind the counter took her order.

"An espresso for here and a double to go, please."

As she stood there sipping the hot, rich brew, she looked past the girl at the cash register and an old friend, situated behind the counter, caught her eye

"Please add a pack of Winstons to the bill."

This was not a time in her life for temperance or denial, she thought to herself. She gathered up the cigarettes and coffee and went back to the college to spend the rest of the afternoon reading the remainder of Slattery's journal.

Upon returning to her rooms, she settled back in her chair, picked up the journal from the lamp table, opening it, determined to finish reviewing it by the time she was scheduled to meet Miller and the others for cocktails. She took the lid from the coffee container, savoring the delightful aroma, setting it down on the table, for the moment, to open the pack of Winstons and light up. She took a long lingering drag and felt some guilt for returning to her vice, but, not very much. She quit, cold turkey, five years ago and would do the same again when the madness stopped. Right now, she would take her pleasures when and where she could.

Jo read, nonstop, through the afternoon. The journal did not vary until she got near the end. At that point, the writing became less precise and tidy and more hurried and undisciplined. Connected thoughts did not follow one to the other. The writing was more random and asked questions rather than drawing conclusions as had been the general rule in the first part of the journal. One page was headed with the query: "Which should be the prevailing question, the origin of man or the origin of man's intellect and knowledge?"

The writings following the heading postulated that Darwinists and the Creationists were pursuing the wrong path in concentrating on the physical aspects of humankind on the planet and should have been directing their studies on the evidence of human knowledge as the hall mark of human evolution. Slattery appeared to have no interest in physical evolution, odd for a geneticist, only with human knowledge and its progression which he tangentially suggested is a function of genetics. The rest of the journal continued in the same vein. No indication of empirical data was put forth, only thoughts and considerations, very speculative in nature carrying forward the possibility of the marriage of genetics and human knowledge. In her mind it was a certainty that Slattery had been contacted by the parties who were behind the Foundation and, in some way reinforced his belief or were the origins of that belief and that this line of research would make him a figure of historical proportions in the field of genetics. A man such as Slattery could not possibly pass up such an opportunity.

Finally, she reached the end and checked her watch. It was just past 6:00 o'clock in the evening. In les than an hour she would be meeting Miller and some of his colleagues for drinks and dinner. She closed the journal, put it back on the table, sank back into the chair and lit her second cigarette of the day. She exhaled and watched the smoke drift lazily through the bright beams of light from the setting sun streaming in through the windows. She thought about Fiona. She would go back to the flat, first thing in the morning and see if she was there or had possibly left a message. She showered and prepared herself for the evening and donned a conservative black cocktail dress and short black jacket. One last calming smoke to facilitate reflecting on the day's events and she would be off to join Miller for cocktails and whatever else the evening brought.

Jo found her way to the Fellows lounge and stopped in the doorway, momentarily, looking for Miller. She surveyed the room. It was one of those old, wonderful, luxuriously decorated and richly appointed rooms which abound at the colleges, but, are hidden away only to be enjoyed by the privileged few, complete with a baby grand off to one side, being softly played by one of the more talented students, setting the mood for the evening. She located Miller standing next to the large, ornate fireplace and moved through the small crowd, attracting admiring glances from the males in attendance while she made her way toward him, picking up a vodka on the rocks as she crossed the room.

"Good evening, Joanna."

Jo nodded her head. "Dr."

Miller took her by the arm and led her to an isolated area of the room.

"I trust that you've found what you're looking for."

Not entirely, but, I'm still looking. One thing I'd like to ask."

"Certainly."

"There's a five day gap in Slattery's day planner from the time of the recorded end of his last vacation trip to France to the time he actually returned to Cambridge. Do you have any idea why?"

No. Frankly, I hadn't realized that fact and of course, once he left the college, no one went back to the records to review any of his goings on."

After that brief exchange, they both dropped the subject and put the Slattery matter aside for the duration of the evening. At the dinner, Miller honored her visit with a toast and she spent a good part of the rest of the night engaged in conversation with a delightful and gracious young man who introduced himself as Jeremy Smith and who very much reminded her of the Peter of old and was about the same age as when they were lovers. His uncanny physical resemblance caused her to feel an attraction to him.

Time sped by much too fast. Soon goodnights were being said and she was being walked back to her residence by the engaging young man who had been her companion for the evening. They walked up the stairs to the landing outside of her door. He clasped her hand and told her how much he had enjoyed her company and conversation at dinner. She felt her emotions running high and fought off the almost irresistible urge to draw him to her and kiss him. She quickly composed herself, thanked him for a wonderful evening and went inside. There was no time for affairs with a man ten years her junior. She couldn't afford such a dalliance, at least not now. In eight hours, she would have to rise and meet what was going to be a challenging day.

CHAPTER NINE

Jo had gone to sleep, on Friday night, with Fiona, the last thing on her mind and woke up, on Saturday morning with Fiona, the first thing on her mind. It was if she had never gone to sleep at all. She wanted to get over to the flat, as soon as possible, check to see if Fiona was there or had left a message and then come back to the college to get through the rest of Slattery's notebooks.

She washed, dressed and hastily made her way to the gate. It was the crack of dawn and the main gate was not yet opened, so, she requested the night porter, who was still on duty, to let her out. The streets were deserted as she walked, leaving the car at the college, the quickest route to the flat, down some back streets and mews which cut a few precious minutes off the time. She arrived at the flat, but, could not immediately tell if the Jag was there as the garage door was closed. She was anxious yet hopeful as she unlocked the door and went in. There was no activity and as far as she could tell, no Fiona.

"Fiona, are you home?". Jo called out. There was unwelcome silence. She took a quick survey of the premises, but, it was obvious that no one had been there. The message machine was blinking "1". She pressed "messages" and listened in anticipation. It was Fiona.

"Jo, if you're there pick up."

There was a pause.

"I'll be back Sunday evening or night, depending. When you get back, sit tight and wait for me till I get there. It's important that we speak, as soon as possible."

The message ended with the familiar tone.

She was relieved that she had received a message from her fiend, but, not so at its cryptic nature. For now, she would go back to the college to complete her work and return to the flat, Sunday morning, to wait for Fiona.

She went back to the college, stopping at the cafe to get another double espresso, to go. She didn't bother with food. This would be one of those days where she would be sustained by caffeine, nicotine and adrenaline.

Back at her rooms, Jo surveyed the remaining box and arranged the notebooks according to date so as to make some sense out of them. The rest of the morning and most of the afternoon was exasperating. There was nothing definitive that added anything to what she already knew about whatever it was in which Slattery was involved. The afternoon was drawing to a close and there wasn't much left to read. She was getting to the final pages in the last notebook that Slattery had left behind. She lit up another cigarette, took a drag and exhaled with a sigh of frustration as she began to examine the remaining entries on the pages before her.

"My meeting at the Village of Saint-Nazair proved both illuminating and exciting", read the first sentence at the top of the page. By referencing the date of the notebook in combination with Slattery's acknowledging a visit to the French village, Jo concluded that this must have been the answer to the question of the missing five days in his vacation itinerary. Her interest spiked. Maybe this was what she was looking for; something to give her an edge in dealing with Slattery. It would be doubtful that he would suspect her background research into his activities. He would probably assume that she would be as ambitious as he and abandon all prudence and restraint in a quest for greatness and notoriety or, perhaps, infamy. She quickened the pace of her reading as Slattery's words started to come alive.

"Much of what I had theorized, was now, not only provable, but, attainable. Who we are and where we come from, as physical beings, are not the important questions. The discovery of what we are capable of, as a race, is the scientific path of inquiry which must be followed if humankind is to reach its potential. The past, if unlocked, will be our future."

That was it. Jo closed the final journal and tossed it back into the box. She grabbed the pack of Winston's and dumped out the last cigarette that was rattling around inside. She looked at it, then crumbled it and put it into the ashtray. She needed air, not tobacco and decided on a walk to clear her head, sort things out and see if she could draw any conclusions. The fresh air smelled good and she would spend the rest of the afternoon sitting by the Cam in the place where she had greeted Fiona, upon her arrival in Cambridge, a week ago, although events made it seem a far longer time than seven days. Things were quiet. It was past tea time and the pubs were empty of those who would be back in a couple of hours to begin their Saturday night of revelry. The sun on her face and the breeze coming off the water felt good. Thoughts were piling on thoughts as she reviewed events and information in her mind. At least she knew that Fiona was safe, but, the reasons for her unusual conduct and the enigmatic telephone message were still troubling loose ends.

Slattery's writings, taken by themselves, were too amorphous for the purpose of drawing any conclusions which is probably why he considered them of no importance and left them behind. But still, they were part of the puzzle, no matter how small. Monday was post time. She would be starting at the Foundation. That would be her first, real opportunity to determine where Slattery's ambitions had taken him.

Before she knew it, it was early evening and people were beginning to filter into the pub. She had forgotten that she had not eaten all day, but, was quickly reminded by the empty feeling and gnawing pain in the pit of her stomach. She would have dinner at The Eagle. That would be a good place to spend some time. It would provide her with food for the soul as well as the body. It was the most famous of all the local pubs, especially to Americans, having been frequented by American fliers stationed near and about Cambridge during World War II. Their patronage of the establishment was evidenced by the multitude of squadron numbers and designations burned into the ceiling for posterity. This gave the pub's past a certain materiality to be experienced by anyone who was fortunate enough to spend some time within its walls.

Jo walked in, found a small table and ordered a large scotch, and a pint of lager. It was one of those days and there would be many more of them to come. She was famished. A steak and Guiness pie would do nicely. As she sat eating her dinner, she remembered how she used to relish coming to this place, as a student, and looking up at the ceiling trying to put herself in the place of the young men who came and went and how many spent the last night of their lives here, before being sent out on a mission from which they would never return. At that time, she, like most, could only wonder. They were merely spectators to history and not the heroes who lived it. It was much the same feeling that she had back in New York about her helplessness after the attack against the World Trade Center. If she had any lingering resentments against Peter for upsetting her life by involving her in the Slattery investigation, this evening, at The Eagle, would be her epiphany and would give her an understanding of the importance of what she was doing. She was no longer a spectator. She was a player. Her doubt turned to appreciation for Peter in giving her a chance to affect events and not merely to be victimized by them.

The pub was becoming crowded, only unlike a week ago, it was filling up with Cambridge students who were arriving for the new session. The European teenagers and tourists had all but disappeared. As she surveyed the crowd, she spotted, on the other side of the room, the young man she met at last night's dinner. She wouldn't go over to say hello. She would be an interloper. He was with a young woman and having to explain her to his companion would only complicate his evening. In seeing him again, she realized that she didn't even get to know him, except for his name, although they conversed, almost exclusively with one another, through most of Friday night. It was not at all like her to exhibit such disinterest in a person and simply associate with them to fulfill a need of the moment. Perhaps, it was her way of avoiding familiarity with a young man who reminded her so much of Peter. It was a comfort to her attributing her behavior to the latter, although she knew, in her heart of hearts that the daily changes in her life circumstances were resulting in noticeable changes in her personality even in a period as short as a week and were bringing out characteristics in her that she never realized were a part of her makeup, but, had been lying dormant, just under the surface, waiting to emerge if the environment was right. The environment, she concluded was right.

She left The Eagle and walked through the streets of Cambridge which, in the darkness and in some of the less commercial areas of the city dominated by its centuries old buildings, cobblestone streets and dim street lights one might be led to believe that they had been transported from the twenty first century into the middle of a scene from the pages of a Victorian mystery novel. Maybe she'd bump into Holmes, she thought. It wasn't that late, so, the main gate of the college wasn't locked. She waved to the night porter as she walked past the office. She wished it was Martin sitting at the desk. She could have used some company. In her room she felt a sense of security, but, also of loneliness and isolation. She wondered what tomorrow would bring and what Fiona had in store for her. As she lay in the dark, waiting for sleep to come, through the open window of the bed chamber she could hear the voices of the people passing by the back gate as they traversed the sidewalks of Cambridge seeking one more place to have a pint. The sound of humanity was welcome, but, also reminded her, in a melancholy way, just how far in the past and irretrievable were the carefree days when she was a student and how just a period of ten years can seem like an eternity.

CHAPTER TEN

It was Sunday morning and Jo packed up in preparation to leave the college. She had gotten about a total of two hours of sleep, waking up at 5:30 A.M. She went down to the entrance, turned in her keys and had the night porter let her out. There had been rain the previous night and some misty precipitation continued to fill the air. She got into the Mini and drove back, in the darkness, to the flat, where, as Fiona's message had commanded, she would sit tight and wait, for what she did not know. The thought was a weight on her and the depressing weather didn't help.

Back at the flat she occupied her mind by going over and over events and the bits of information that she became privy to, doing her best to make some sense of it all. She had no desire to do any more review for tomorrow when she would start at the Foundation. What preparation she had done would have to be adequate. Besides, that would not be her true purpose for being there. Tomorrow! That's when it would all start. That's when her commitment would be put to the test.

She heard the whistle of the kettle that she had put on the stove, went into the kitchen and prepared a cup of tea. Despite the gloomy weather, she went out to the balcony to sit and think about her conversation with Miller and what she had read in Slattery's notes. Miller had warned her that Slattery was leading her on to serve his own purpose. But, she would have to discount some of that warning as Miller was unaware of her now true purpose for associating with the Foundation. It had all changed after her meeting with Peter. In a true sense, she, not Slattery, was in control.

She recalled Miller's irritation when telling of his final encounter with Slattery. What was it he said? That Slattery was interested in "panspermia and the origins of human knowledge". She was familiar with that theory. It stated that life did not begin on Earth; that it began elsewhere in the solar system or, perhaps, elsewhere in the universe and was brought here by meteors or comets that impacted our planet and deposited DNA of some sort. Or, possibly sent by intelligent life from some far distant planet. The Mars rock, found a few years ago, has been cited as an example, although whether or not it contained evidence of microscopic, primitive life is disputed. But, a random distribution of primitive life wouldn't provide a basis for the genetic study of the origins of human knowledge as stated by Slattery. Evolution and origin has always been a problem in the field. Changes are attributed to random mutations, but, this is simplistic and explains nothing. Also, the apparent lack of specimens or fossils of transitional species constitutes a broadside fired against Darwin. The Creationists tend to go back to the explanation repeated, by rote, in parochial school, "Who made us? God made us". This is a concept made more palatable by re-naming it Intelligent Design or something of the like; not a much better explanation and if reflected upon, it is a term which raises even more interesting and exotic questions. Although Slattery was not interested in physical evolution, it would seem that he would run into the same conundrums. Unless, Jo thought, what Slattery was doing was not speculation, but, that he had something tangible or material on which to base his work at the Foundation. Perhaps, he had something in hand, by which he could unlock the past; something more than a theory. But, if that was the truth, then how did she fit in? Certainly, at some point, Slattery would have to disclose something, if not all, of the real purpose for having her join the Foundation. She knew that she couldn't sit idly by and wait for him to divulge his secrets in his own time. She would have to press the matter. She had a job to do and time would be critical. As for now, her concern turned to Fiona, where she was and why. What was the importance of making sure that she would be there, at the flat, when Fiona returned? No more thinking. She took refuge in the restful bliss of Fiona's extensive, classical CD collection and spent the rest of the afternoon letting the music fill her mind and watching the world go by from her vantage point on the balcony.

It was the end of the afternoon and Jo heard the key in the door. Fiona was earlier than expected. She entered the apartment throwing her briefcase and overnight bag in the corner.

"Jo, I'm glad you're here."

Her words were spoken in an obvious sense of relief.

"I got your message", responded Jo.

Without saying anything further, Fiona walked from the door directly to the bar.

"Scotch?"

"Please."

"Rocks?"

"Yeah."

Fiona turned around, appearing anxious, drinks in hand. She gave one to Jo and sat down on the sofa, next to her. Fiona took a long drink and set the glass on the coffee table in front of them. Jo sat there, glass in hand, forgetting that she was even holding it, being preoccupied with Fiona and the revelation or revelations that she had in store. Fiona took another drink and looked sternly at Jo.

"I don't know how else to say this."

There was a pause and Jo knew that there was bad news.

"Peter is dead."

Jo sat there motionless. Fiona's words didn't seem real. She had the sensation of being paralyzed, her mind swimming and detached from her physical body trying, at that moment, to comprehend the incomprehensible. Peter, dead. How could that be? She looked at Fiona, mystified.

"I don't understand, when did this happen?"

"Take a drink of your scotch, try to calm yourself and I'll explain."

Jo took a sip of her drink, the clinking of the ice cubes in the glass being the only sound interrupting the momentary quite as Fiona sat waiting to unfold her story on the matters relating to Peter.

"Peter was hit by a car."

"Where?"

"In London, on Thursday night."

"How did it happen?", Jo asked in a desperate and impatient tone.

"He was crossing a street in Soho. He was struck and killed instantly."

"Did they get the driver?"

"No. It was a hit and run."

"What about a description of the car, a license number, anything?"

"No, nothing. It was a backstreet and a couple of people arrived on the scene just after it happened, but, there were no witnesses."

Fiona took Jo by the hand. "I'm so sorry", she said in a sinking voice, trying to console her friend and at the same time, overcoming her own grief at the loss of Peter.

Fiona's news about Peter made Jo's blood run cold. *Was it her worst fear coming true? Could Peter's death be connected to his recruitment of her to gather information against Slattery?* Peter seemed to be so sure of his anonymity in his clandestine activities. And yet, the questions kept presenting themselves. *Could she have done something that doomed Peter?* Perhaps, her afternoon of spying on the Foundation was foolish. *And what of the young man whom she had encountered?* Maybe his coming upon her was not as benign a circumstance as it seemed to be. No, she concluded. Of course not. She was reacting badly to the news of Peter's death. Control was called for. She had to pull herself together. *What was she to do about Slattery and the Foundation?* As her mind settled down and rationality began to reassert itself, she was faced with the curious reality that, apparently, Fiona had been called to London upon Peter's death. That was the reason for her absence and the hasty departure from the flat. Some questions needed answering.

"How did you find out about the accident?", asked Jo.

"I got a phone call."

"From one of Peter's friends?"

Jo felt that the question was moot. Her instincts were telling her that Fiona had not heard from friends, but, from some other source. She wasn't sure how she wanted the question answered. It would simplify her life if it actually was a friend who broke the news, but, the hope of any opportunity to discover the secret of Slattery and the foundation would be dashed. She would no longer be a player, but, again be reduced to a helpless spectator of events. That was unacceptable. Fiona's answer allayed her fears.

"No. I didn't hear from one of Peter's friends. I heard from one of Peter's associates at the agency."

"What are you saying?"

"I'm saying that I've not been totally candid with you and for that I apologize, but, it was necessary under the circumstances."

"So, you were in league with Peter, is that it?"

Jo burst out in laughter. It was the laughter of anxiety stemming from a combination of the loss of Peter and yet another revelation in the many twists and turns her life had taken as of recent days. But, the irony of it all actually provided some relief and a distraction from her personal sorrow.

"And to think that all of this time, since my meeting with him, I've been feeling guilt because I thought that I was the one engaging in the charade. I guess I was. But, it seems, I've got company."

"Let me explain", implored Fiona. "I am an investment counselor. That much is true. But, I use the profession and the access it gives me to trace the assets of the bad guys. I search out leads to try and find out where the world's assorted despots and dictators keep their stash. As of late I've been I've been tracking money transfers of suspected terrorist organizations and their operatives. I did some work on Slattery and the Foundation, but, that was a dead end. Their trail is much too intricate."

"How did you get involved in all of this?"

"When we graduated and after you went back to the States, there was the ususal government recruiting going on. Peter and I interviewed, sort of as a lark and one thing led to another. Peter went with government intelligence and I worked on the periphery using my business as a cover for my investigations."

"Why were you called when Peter was killed?"

"Because of my relationship with you and the fact that Peter had recruited you. The whole thing is an unusually fortunate sequence of events, a series of coincidences, serendipity or whatever name you want to give to it. Both Peter and I were involved in our work for the government. Peter's focus was on the investigation of Slattery and the Foundation. Slattery called you to assist him in his work because, apparently your research dovetailed with what he was doing. This plus the fact that you were an outsider, not part of the Cambridge community, enhanced your eligibility to be picked by him. We had been trying to get one of our people into the Foundation, but, never had any success. If we knew that you would be the person for the job, we would have contacted you, ourselves. I'm sure that Peter had explained, to you, that we were continuously monitoring Slattery as best we could. We never got much, but, when we detected the letter, to you, we knew that this was our opportunity. The rest, as they say, is history. After that everything fell into place which, for us, is a rarity."

"Then the plan will go forward?", Jo asked.

"Absolutely."

"I'm relieved to hear that."

"So, you're eager to get on with it?"

"I am.'

"I know how you feel. When you start into this stuff you're a bit shaky about the whole thing. But, then it grabs you. It consumes you and you can't get enough of it. There's a special excitement to it and nothing else will do."

Jo knew that Fiona was right. The process that her friend was describing was happening to her. Intrigue, not genetics, was rapidly becoming the driving force in her life. She was shattered by the loss of Peter, but, had to approach his death in a pragmatic way. There were some important questions that needed answers.

"Fiona, is there any chance that Peter's death is connected to the investigation of the Foundation? You know, a warning shot across the bow or a means to get me to back off and go away. Even though I'm the one going into the Foundation, Peter might be a less high profile target, but, the message would still get through. It would be a form of test to see if I was associated with him in a professional way. The thinking would be, that if I was, I would be scared off and if I wasn't, then they could still use me."

"That can't be ruled out, but, it's highly unlikely. Slattery and those behind him, have too good a thing going to involve themselves in violence and thus far, to the best of our knowledge, they haven't. It would be stupid to expose themselves like that and they aren't stupid people. That's not to say that you should drop your guard. You never know how they're thinking and there's always that chance."

"What's your position in this whole matter?"

"It's been decided that Peter won't be replaced. There isn't anyone that can act as your contact without creating suspicion. No one, that is, except me. Rather than reporting what you find to Peter, you'll be advising me."

Fiona's surprising declarations had temporarily distracted Jo from her sadness at the news of Peter's death. But, her thoughts were drawn back to the inescapable fact that Peter was gone. She would not see him tomorrow or next week or ten years from now, She would never see him again. That was the realization and emptiness that had to be reckoned with and even though their romance died a long time ago, she really did still love him in a deeper and more enduring way.

The two friends spent some considerable time, that evening, discussing and remembering Peter. It was good therapy. Finally, the conversation drifted back to the matter at hand. Jo related her the happenings of her meeting with Miller, her findings, what there was of them, during her weekend at the college and her observations at the Foundation during her afternoon drive. Fiona was particularly interested in the reference to Saint-Nazaire and the lost five days. She posed a question to Jo.

"There was nothing at all which gave any clue for his trip to Saint-Nazaire?"

"No, nothing."

"Then maybe it was just a place of convenience and somewhere Slattery thought was safe where he wouldn't be detected", surmised Fiona.

"That's probably part of it, but, I can't help thinking there's more."

Jo reflected on her previous thoughts as to people who keep notes and memos and how these things come back to haunt those people. The Saint-Nazaire reference might prove itself to be one of those situations. She continued the conversation.

"I think there was a reason, or a purpose, to have Slattery go there."

"You don't believe it was his choice?"

"No. I think that meeting was used to seal the deal by those who wanted Slattery to head up the Foundation and there was something unique about that village that had some importance to that end."

"Maybe a trip is in order", suggested Fiona.

"I'm not going to be able to fit it in. Tomorrow is the start with Slattery. I want to focus on trying to find out what the hell is going on out at the compound."

"Not you. Me. I'll go."

"Won't you call attention to yourself? That's the last thing we need."

"No. I'll go via Paris. I make frequent business trips there and there's no reason that one more trip to France would raise suspicions. I'll stay in Paris for a couple of days and take a side trip to Saint-Nazaire to see what I can find out."

"Good. I'm sure there's something there. When would you go?"

"Tomorrow. When you start at the Foundation."

"How long do you think you'll be away?"

"I'll give myself the business week and be back sometime during the weekend, depending on what happens. We can keep in touch as long as we're careful about what we say."

"So, tomorrow it all begins."

"It does."

CHAPTER ELEVEN

It was 6:00 o'clock, Monday morning. The weather was lousy. The sky was gray and oppressive, the clouds were low, there was a chill in the air and the intensity of the rain had increased since yesterday. Summer was on its way out and it was becoming England, again. Jo and Fiona shared coffee and breakfast, but, conversation was minimal. Both were caught up in the thoughts of the week and their respective tasks to be completed.

"Well, I've got to get started", Fiona remarked as she got up from the kitchen table. I've got one hell of a drive to get to Dover and this bloody weather isn't going to help. I'm going to have to stay over and leave for France tomorrow."

"It looks like you might be away longer than the business week", observed Jo.

"Maybe. I'll keep in touch and let you know."

Fiona gathered her bags and left to start off on her odyssey to, what they both hoped, would be some revelations to be found in the Village of Saint - Nazaire. Now, there was no Peter and temporarily, there would be no Fiona. Jo felt isolated and exposed. No time for emotion or self absorption, she decided. There were things to do and plans to hatch and it would all begin the minute she walked out the door.

It was 7:00 o'clock. The anticipated problems with traffic and weather dictated that an early start would be necessary. Jo stuffed her work notes, that she had brought with her, into a briefcase and made her way downstairs to the Mini. The rain had increased. She crossed her fingers that this wasn't an indicator of the days events to come. She made her way out of Cambridge and left the road congestion behind her as she finally made her way on the road to the compound, listening to the sound of the rain beating on the metal roof of the car and the methodical, almost mesmerizing, thumping of the windshield wipers as they swept back and forth. It was all she could do to concentrate and peer through the foggy air while, at the same time, remembering to stay on the left side of the road and not send herself and some other hapless motorist into oblivion. At last, she reached the turnoff, went down the road to the Foundation and through the gate, courtesy, once again, of Jack who instructed her to go straight to the lab building.

She drove down the dirt path toward the white wooden structure, Mini bumping along the way in the ruts of the unpaved surface some deep enough to swallow up a wheel and cause muddy water to spray over the windshield, defeating the best efforts of the cars wipers to keep her view from being obscured. Through the rain, the fog, the wipers and the mess, she saw Slattery waiting at the laboratory doorway. He was motionless and seemed pensive at her arrival, a contrast to the exuberant personality he exhibited at their initial meeting. It was apparent that he was as anxious as she was at the reality that she was actually now a part of the Foundation and all that may entail. Jo parked the Mini and hastily exited the car, running to the entrance to try and avoid getting wet in the steady downpour. Good mornings were exchanged and Slattery led Jo to her lab. Everything was as he had promised; a full complement of brand new lab equipment, all state of the art and all to her specifications to accomplish the somewhat limited purpose that they had originally discussed during their introductory meeting.

"I trust that you find everything in good order", queried Slattery.

"Everything is excellent, actually somewhat more than I'd expected. You've really outdone yourself, Doctor."

"We don't cut corners around here. If you need anything further, anything at all, please don't hesitate to ask. I'm going back to the house to catch up on a few things, so, I'll leave you to familiarize yourself and get started. I'll call on you later."

Slattery turned, exited the lab, popped open a large, black umbrella and walked toward the main house. Jo watched as he made his way through the rain and over the uneven and muddy ground. As he passed the concrete lab, he stopped and briefly took a look at the door, before he continued on. She harkened back to the altercation that she observed between Slattery and Jack while she was observing the compound from her vantage point on the road overlooking the grounds. The fact that Slattery checked the door was an indication that Jack might be a weak link in the day to day activities of the Foundation, at least, as to security within the gates. Perhaps, he was careless in his duties and that the mistake he made in leaving the door ajar, might very well be repeated. She would have to be alert to take advantage, if such an opportunity arose.

Her section of the lab building was isolated from other areas of the building and prevented her from easily interacting with the lab technicians. This, no doubt, was intentional on Slattery's part as he was probably still dubious as to whether or not she could be drawn in to his master plan so that he could gain the necessary confidence in her loyalty. That was fine. Right now, she was more interested in taking advantage of being in the compound and taking the opportunity to look around. At least the location of her area with its windows gave her a good vantage point to see most of the activity that was taking place outside.

By chance and luck, she could see the enigmatic brick buildings. As she focused her attention at that area her attention was caught by what was parked under an overhang on the side of one of the buildings. It was a yellow motorcycle. It was THE yellow motorcycle; the one that the young man was riding the day that she was spying on the compound. A sense of alarm came over her.

Who was he? What was he doing here? Did he know that she was associated with the Foundation? It was as sure as hell that he was going to know of her presence as soon as he spotted that damned red Mini parked outside. *How much jeopardy was she in?* She was at the mercy of Slattery while she was on the grounds of the compound. That had always been in the back of her mind, but, now the reality of it became all too real.

She didn't have long to think about it, when she suddenly saw a vehicle coming up the path. It was a black Land rover and as it got closer she could see that, sitting inside, were the same two men that she had observed in the vehicle when it passed her in front of the tea room, last week. No doubt it was the same Rover and men that Fiona had seen when they were returning from the first meeting with Slattery. She also glimpsed two women, also Asian, in the back seat. As they pulled up to the area in front of the brick buildings, her attention was called to the main house where she saw a figure exit the front door. It was Jack He walked over to the Rover and began conversing with the two men. The discussion was short and one of the men handed Jack a small black briefcase. He opened it, took out a red file folder, quickly thumbed through it and nodded his approval to the man standing before him. The women were assisted out of the Rover where they stood, with Jack, waiting as the two men climbed into the vehicle and drove back down the road, disappearing into the misty gloom. Jack and the women turned and proceeded toward one of the buildings. Suddenly there was a short gust of wind and the rain coat of one of the women blew open, for a moment. The woman grabbed the fluttering garment and gathered her arms around it to make sure it did not open again. But, it was too late. Jo had seen what was not supposed to be seen. Pregnant! The young woman was pregnant and in all likelihood, so was her companion. Jo thought back to the mystery person opening the door when she was observing from the road. No doubt it was another such woman who was residing at the compound.

"So, that's it", Jo thought to herself. She was right in thinking that the buildings were residences, but, not, apparently, just for the staff. That was the answer to the question. But, another had been raised. Who were these women and why were they brought to the compound? Certainly, there was the possibility that the answer may lie in the fact that part of the activity of the Foundation involved itself in the field of in vitro fertilization. But, that answer seemed too simple and didn't ring true and besides, Slattery never indicated that human experimentation had anything to do with his work. However, operations of the Foundation were too clandestine to support the obvious or any representations or assurances that Slattery may have made to her. She continued to watch as Jack left the residence and headed back to the main house, carrying, with him, the small black briefcase. How she would love to get a look at that file.

Facts were coming to light, but, they were fragments; pieces scattered here and there. There was some central truth which would pull them all together, but, that truth was elusive. Only a little less than two weeks had elapsed since she had arrived in Cambridge. That was enough time for her to conclude that whatever Slattery and his benefactors were up to had probably been going on for a considerable period of time, years in fact, and pressures had caused it to be put on the fast track to get to some sort of a conclusion. That was probably why she was recruited. It was not something that they wanted to do. It was something that they had to do. Right now it was the first morning of the first day at the Foundation and all she could do was to proceed with her assigned work, knowing that this was not what she was there for and hoping that the urgency that was driving Slattery would force his hand into giving her the information that she was looking for. So, for now, there was nothing to do but commence to set up her lab space and continue with the charade.

A few uneventful hours passed and it was approaching noon. There was a break in the weather and although the Sun had not broken through, the sky was brighter and the oppressive rain had stopped. She had been involved in her work for what seemed a relatively short period of time, when the door to the lab building opened. It was Jack. He strode over to her assigned area of the building

"Dr. Russo."

"Yes, Jack?"

"The Doctor would like you to join him in the main house."

"Now?"

"If you please."

"That's fine."

Jack escorted Jo out the door and they both walked over to the main house with her leading the way and Jack following closely behind. She found that her discomfort with Jack's presence was still her overwhelming reaction to him. They entered the house and found Slattery sitting on a large, white, leather chair, opposite an equally white leather sofa. Before him, on the glass top coffee table was an elaborate tray of tea and sandwiches, of some sort. He quickly rose and turned around to greet Jo.

"Good afternoon, Joanna."

"Good afternoon, Doctor"

"Please have a seat", offered Slattery as he gestured toward the sofa.

Jo sat down, opposite Slattery.

"I know it's early for tea, but, I've never been a slave to convention. Would you care for something?"

"Just tea will be fine."

Slattery's attention was focused on pouring the tea as he asked Jo a question.

"Tell me. What is your overview, your understanding, of genetic memory?"

"How do you mean?"

"Do you believe that it's a viable concept."

"You mean more than a theory."

"Yes."

"Well, it has a validity of sorts, when applied in certain experiments; simple responses in lower life forms and the like. It's termed genetic memory, but, it's more in the nature of acquired characteristics or behavior. But, you already know that. I take it that your question implies something more."

"Yes. Yes it does. Tell me, what is your belief in the possibility that genetic memory or, combined with intellectual capacity and output could be transferred from generation to generation at the genetic level?"

"I don't hold beliefs in such things, Doctor. I rely on the observation of empirical data. Your question would be more aptly put to a philosopher."

"Very good, indeed, Joanna. That is precisely the answer that I would expect from a scientist such as yourself. A few short years ago that is what I, myself, would have said."

"But, not now?"

"No, not now."

"What changed your mind?"

"Ah, as always, to the point. But, sometimes a direct response is not the most constructive way to answer a question. Let me suggest, instead, some things for your consideration. Would you concede that the recorded history of man is filled with unsolved mysteries and contradictions?"

"Of course. There are many in our own field."

"No, no. I don't mean the mundane questions of science that we plod along to decipher, day after day, by means of our precious and unyielding scientific method. I'm talking about things that seem to be inexplicable, almost mythological, the explanation of which has been lost in the murkiness of the past, but when looked at in a new way in a new light, the cloak of mystery is slowly peeled away. Are you a student of history? I mean ancient history, archeological history, or for that matter, bible history?"

"I can't say that I'm a student of these things, but, I've read some."

"Then you're aware that there is an historic record that from time to time things present themselves which are not easily explained if they are explicable at all. Artifacts of a certain nature have been found or represented on stone relief or painted on walls which should not have been there, because it has always been our belief that these things were the product of the science of the last couple of hundred years and not the creations of those who preceded us by thousands of years. But, like it or not and despite the protestations and ridicule of those in the scientific world who will not see, the evidence is there. I'm sure that in your readings you've come across matters that have piqued your curiosity."

"That's true. I've read of things such as the so-called 'Baghdad Battery' and gold Colombian artifacts that resemble modern jet aircraft. The reading provided entertainment and some interest, but, not more than that."

Jo was being careful not to include the inventions and concepts of da Vinci in her conversation with Slattery lest she raise any suspicions, in him, as to her intentions concerning her association with the Foundation.. Slattery picked up on his thoughts with regard to those things which he considered historical evidence of that which, apparently, was the central focus of his work, although he had yet to come out and simply state it. Slattery continued his thoughts.

"Even religious texts lend themselves to the proposition. Many who believe the scriptures and the word of the Bible have concluded that the description of the Arc of the Covenant is consistent with it being a capacitor, storing electricity and discharging it if the Arc was violated. Surely such a creation would be out of place as to its existence at that time in history. If one accepts that premise, then the question presents itself as to how such a thing could exist. This brings us to the, shall we say, intellectual fork in the road. Do we attribute it to the natural or to the supernatural. The supernatural requires only belief and nothing more. The natural requires an explanation and evidence to buttress that explanation. Even Christ, himself, might have accomplished his miracles, not because of his divinity, but, because he was a man possessed of knowledge and usable intellect thousands of years ahead of his time and for that matter, our time."

"Surely you're joking", Jo responded, incredulously.

"On the contrary, I'm quite serious", Slattery responded, showing some irritation with Jo's reaction to what he had said. "Through observation, one could postulate that there has been an ebb and flow of evidence of human development, throughout the ages. Some civilizations reached their high point only to sink into the status of present day underdeveloped countries racked by poverty, hunger, war and pestilence, where the Four Horsemen of the Apocalypse are not a dire warning for the future, but, an everyday reality to be endured. Some have been lost to the ages. There has been a lack of consistency. Advancement then regression. Knowledge found and lost. If one had the key, the secret, the means by which to unlock the potential of the human intellect which has shown itself only sporadically during the time of written human history and before, human achievement would accelerate at a pace undreamed. That which would have taken many hundreds of years would be accomplished in a generation. Particle physics, anti-gravity propulsion systems even the solution to interstellar travel; all of those things which seem so distant could be accomplished in a human lifespan."

Jo considered what he said and was prepared to ask him if he had the key about which he spoke, but, before she could the front door opened. She turned around to see that the person entering was the young man that she had encountered on the road, last week. How often had she used and heard the expression of someone's blood running cold? She now knew what it truly meant. He saw Jo and stood in the doorway, momentarily as if to size up the situation before he reacted. He stepped into the living room, walking toward Slattery and her but did not acknowledge Jo as someone that he was familiar with.

"Ah, Piero! Please come in", greeted Slattery.

Piero proceeded to where they were seated, continuing to exercise welcome discretion as to his recognition of Jo.

"Let me introduce you to Dr. Russo. She'll be here for a while, helping me with my work."

"Very pleased to meet you Doctor."

He gave her a friendly but brief handshake.

"Nice meeting you Piero".

Piero turned away from Jo and directed himself to Slattery.

"The rain's let up and I'll be going into town. Do you have anything for me to do?"

"No, nothing that I can think of."

"Good. Then I'll be on my way. It's been nice meeting you, Dr Russo."

He riveted his eyes on hers.

"If I can be of any assistance to you for anything, anything at all, while you're here, I'm at your service."

She pulled herself from his stare.

"Thank you very much Piero. I'll keep that in mind."

The young man's words implied something more than just polite banter. She would have to wait and see what developed as far as her further endeavors with him were concerned. She was sure that he was more than he seemed to be. For now, she was grateful that he didn't mention their previous encounter. The circumstances of their introduction, by Slattery, also told her that he had not mentioned it, previously, to him. Apparently, unlike Jack, he exercised some independence from Slattery. There was much to learn about Piero and she had to learn it quickly.

"I'm afraid that I'm going to have to cut our conversation short. I have some things that I have to attend to."

"That's fine, Doctor. I have to get back to the lab and finish setting up."

"Do you need anything else?"

"No. I have everything that I need to get started."

" Good. I'll look in on you later. Think about what I said this afternoon."

Jo didn't make any comment as she left the house and started her short walk back to the lab. She had more elements to consider after her meeting with Slattery. But, the picture was still fragmented. The elusive thing which would bring it all together was still missing.

Back at the lab, Jo continued to busy herself. The other technicians reminded her of drones who kept, slavishly, to their respective tasks and were resistant to any attempt, by her, to engage in even passing conversation on the rare times that she was even close enough to talk to hem. Their guarded attitude seemed to result from a combination of fear and distrust and was disappointing as to any hope that these people could be a source of information as to things that they may have seen or heard. Slattery had disciplined his people well.

The rest of her working day proved to be uneventful and had come to an end. It was a relief to get into the Mini. The car became an instant refuge, giving her some comfort even while she was still within the confines of the compound. As she left the grounds, through the gate, she encountered Piero returning on his motorcycle. She slowed down as they passed each other, intending to briefly speak to him over her puzzlement at why, when Slattery introduced them, that afternoon, he had not acknowledged their previous meeting the prior week. She called to him, but, to her surprise, his only acknowledgement was a wave to her after which he kept on going. It was obvious that he intended to keep their relationship at arm's length, at least in the vicinity of the compound. She had to find out the reason, but, whatever it was, it took the pressure off her and gave her confidence that Piero would not do or say something that would give her a problem with Slattery.

The drive back to the flat was quicker than she anticipated. The traffic wasn't bad and the weather was vastly improved over the muck that it was in the morning. When she finally got back, she had a sense of what a lifeless place the flat was without the presence of Fiona. Back in New York, she relished the privacy and solitude of her apartment, but, here and under these circumstances, she felt a loneliness. She settled in for the evening and picked at some food, abandoned that and poured herself a cognac. She still had a lot of leftover energy from the day and needed something to occupy her mind. She found one of Fiona's cigarette packs, opened it, took one out and lit up. The da Vinci book was sitting on top of the sideboard. She took it, laid it on the coffee table, sat down on the sofa and began leafing through it as she sipped the soothing cognac. What had they missed? What had they not thought of? Was there anything else in the book which referred to something involving the Foundation? And then it hit her. In concentrating on hidden meanings and clues, they had overlooked the obvious. The Foundation group was fond of naming its organizations after things daVinci. So, what about the Foundation, itself? Could it also have been named after some reference to daVinci only more obscure and circumspect. She anxiously turned to the index and moved her finger, rapidly, down the column of words until she got to the S's. She continued scanning the column only more slowly and carefully; "Salai", "Saint Jerome", "School of Athens", "Self-portrait", "Seneca". Serpentine Curve".

"That's it! That's got to be it!", she exclaimed out loud, only Fiona wasn't there to hear her.

She turned to the page that was cited next to the term and rapidly went through the text until she found what was no more than a sentence in a book that contained over four hundred pages. The term stated a philosophy of artistic creation of the Renaissance. The concept was summed up where it was said that "the spirit of the painter transferred itself into an image of the spirit of God" The implications of using this concept as the basis for naming the Foundation were profound. The idea that Slattery and those who supported him, were on the brink of something that could change the course of human history was both fascinating and frightening. The secrecy with which the Foundation did its work, the heavy financial support from governments known and unknown and the hypothetical proposition which formed the basis of Slattery's afternoon presentation, to her, gave some credence to that supposition. But, this had to be more than just some conventional or, for that matter, unconventional breakthrough in genetics. If one used as part of their working theory that the philosophical concept of the Serpentine Curve had, in fact, a meaningful application to the work of the Foundation, which one could deduce, with a certain degree of validity, given the other da Vinci reference, it could be implied that the Serpentine Foundation was trying to create something, perhaps someone unique and unlike that which had ever existed. Was such a conclusion a quantum leap? Possibly. But, there was a certain logic to it and other explanations or considerations didn't seem to fit. What was it that Holmes said? "Eliminate the impossible and what remains, however improbable, must be the truth."

This would have to be the theory under which she would operate to focus her investigation in the coming days. She would have to convince Fiona and that would not be an easy thing to do. Fond thoughts of Peter passed through her mind. He would be proud of her, she concluded, with a warm satisfaction.

Jo realized that she had been so absorbed in her thoughts and research that she had failed to check the message machine. It was blinking. She pressed the play button. It was Fiona.

"Jo, made it to London. I'll be on my way to France, tomorrow and then on to Paris. I'll see you when I see you. Take care."

That was it. She probably wouldn't hear from her friend again until she returned from her trip. She was eager to relate her theory to Fiona as to the Foundation's activities and hoped that her trip to Saint-Nazaire would provide something to affirm that theory.

She was wound up from the day's events and knew that sleep, tonight, would be difficult. One more cognac and then an attempt to get some rest. She had to figure out what her next step would be. In the back of her mind, she knew that the two women that she had seen enter the compound were instrumental in whatever it was that was the object of Slattery's obsession. That was deeply troubling and gave her a renewed sense of urgency in accomplishing what she had been asked to do. Peter was counting on her and she could not fail him.

CHAPTER TWELVE

Tuesday morning came around. It was to be Jo's second day at the Foundation and she was eager to get out to the compound. Armed with her deductions, she now had a path to follow in her efforts to determine Slattery's activities. She hurried down to the Mini, which she had parked in the garage in Fiona's absence, got in and turned the key. She was greeted by a rapid series of clicks. Again. This time the clicking slowed down and diminished. Again. This time silence.

"Shit!"

Frustrated, she grabbed her cell phone and called Slattery to let him know her problem. Luck was with her and Slattery answered. She was spared the added irritation of having to deal with Jack. He assured her that he understood and suggested sending Piero to collect her and bring her to the compound. She accepted the offer. It would get her to work and give her some time alone with the enigmatic, young man. Perhaps, some questions could be cleared up. She put in a call to the rental agency to pick up and repair the Mini. Now there was nothing to do but wait. It wasn't too long before she heard the familiar sound of the engine and saw the bright yellow motorcycle coming down the street. He pulled up to where Jo was standing, in front of the open garage door.

"Buongiorno, Dottoressa", he shouted out over the noise of the motorcycle engine, as he pulled up.

"Buongiorno, Piero. We're speaking Italian today?"

"A beautiful language, for a beautiful woman."

Jo lowered her head, cocked her eyebrow and looked, suspiciously, at him, out of the corner of her eye. She couldn't help but be flattered by his comment as well as impressed by his aura of self confidence which belied his young age.

"Come. We must go"

As she approached, he handed her the extra helmet.

"I appreciate this, Piero. I hope that it isn't too much trouble."

"Not at all. it's my pleasure. I know that you have questions, but, we can talk later. Right now, Dr. Slattery is waiting."

She swung her leg over the back fender, settled in and grabbed on to Piero as they sped off for the compound. Mercifully, there was no rain this morning and the ride was exhilarating although she always had it on her mind that she must have some time with Piero alone and away from the compound and Slattery. His comment, to her, indicated that he wanted to talk to her and she was sure that, whatever he had to say, she was anxious to hear.

The ride to the Foundation came to an end much too quickly. They arrived at the entrance and Piero lifted a flap on the call box revealing a series of buttons and a small glass plate. He punched in a code and pressed his thumb on the plate. Jo realized that she was probably right about the box, next to the door, on the second lab building and that all secure areas on the compound required finger-print identification for access. Breaking in without some exotic high tech equipment and the knowledge as to it's use would be unlikely, if not impossible. They proc-eeded to the lab building where Slattery was waiting, standing in the doorway, never taking his eyes off them as they approached.

"Good morning, sorry about your car. I hope that you found Piero's motorcycle satisfactory."

"It was very enjoyable."

"Good. Piero, would you be good enough to drive Dr. Russo back, at the end of the day?"

"It would be my pleasure, if it is alright with the Doctor."

"That's fine, Piero and thanks for the lift."

Slattery escorted Jo into the lab.

"Piero seems to be a very nice young man. Where did you find him?"

"He was living with his parents, in China. They were archaeologists and were killed in an unfortunate accident. When I joined the group that established the Foundation, I had occasion to visit China and found him there. I made arrangements to take him under my wing and bring him back to Cambridge. I thought that England would be a more suitable place for him."

Slattery's story, about Piero, just didn't ring true. It was too pat and allowed Piero's past to remain murky. It did however explain the accent that she detected when she first met him. It was Chinese. She just didn't make the connection, at the time. Slattery's explanation was also an indication that he was not reluctant to openly talk about the Chinese connection. But, why not? That fact was certainly something that he couldn't keep secret, from her now that she could observe the activity in the compound. And as Peter had told her, the Chinese participation was well known to both the British and American governments although not widely publicized. The real question was how deep did the support go and for what purpose.

Piero and Slattery's explanation of him, added to the puzzle. Even though she and the young man had interacted for a very short period of time, on a couple of occasions, Piero, who Slattery had described as his ward, was the opposite of her former professor. He was bold, witty, charming and continental in manner in spite of his youth. He was the antithesis of Slattery even though he seemed to live a limited existence, attached as he was, to the Foundation. She didn't know what to make of him.

Slattery excused himself and turned his attention to one of the Asian technicians and had a few words with him. She could not hear what was being said, but, noticed the technician glance at her as if in response to a comment by Slattery. It gave her an uncomfortable feeling and was a further reminder that, no matter how affable her former mentor was in his behavior towards her, this was not a friendly place. This was a fact that she had to keep paramount in her mind in whatever she said or did.

Jo tried to settle in for the day and start organizing the work that Slattery had planned for them. It was difficult for her to concentrate on the assigned task at hand. She was always looking, searching for anything that would add something to what she already knew or had speculated regarding the Foundation and its mission. But, she didn't know enough and speculation was not hard evidence. What she had begun to realize that she was not retained by Peter and his governmental superiors for mere fact finding. She was there to bring Slattery and his colleagues down and to stop the work of the Foundation. This was not explicitly said, but, she had no doubt that this was to be the final outcome.

Her relative isolation in the lab allowed her to take some time consider what was presented to her by Slattery. Although his vision of genetic memory seemed, at least on the surface, to be expansive, she could not help but think that it was, in fact, myopic and limited. He saw gains in the field of science and a future crafted according to his values and the values of those who supported him. It was a certainty that military superiority was a large part of the equation and both the American and British governments had come to the same conclusion.

But, what if Slattery and company had miscalculated? What if the person or persons who would possess the intellectual capacity or collective memory or whatever one chose to call it, would be unwilling to play the Foundation's game? It was and is characteristic of Slattery to be consummately egotistical and presumptuous enough to believe that he could control and manipulate the situation. Perhaps his creation, rather than fulfilling his aspirations to become ruler of the world, or something akin to it, would turn on him much in the manner that the creation of another famous doctor, this one of fictional fame, turned on him.

CHAPTER THIRTEEN

Earlier that same day the phone rang in a room of an intimate, elegant hotel located in St. James Place in the heart of London. Fiona rolled over, barely awake and picked up the receiver.

"Hello."

"This is your wake up call Miss Clark. It's seven o'clock."

"Thank you."

No sooner did she hang up, put her legs over the edge of the bed and her feet on the floor, then there was a knock on the door..

"Yes?", she called out.

"Room service", indicated the person on the other side of the door.

She got up, slipped on a robe and went over to open the door knowing that it would be Tommy, one of the veteran members of the staff whom she had gotten to

SERPENTINE ENIGMA

know from the years of using this particular establishment as a stopover on her innumerable trips to the continent.

"Morning, Miss Clark. Nice to have you back."

"Good morning Tommy. Come in."

"Got your usual, toast, coffee, orange juice and,....."

He reached down to the bottom rack of the cart

"Your Telegraph."

"Perfect."

"Anything else, Miss Clark?"

"Nothing here, but, I'd appreciate it if you'd ask the concierge to make the usual arrangements to garage the Jag for a few days."

"Very good. I'll see to it immediately."

After setting out the breakfast, Tommy left with his cart and a handsome gratuity.

Fiona checked the clock on the bedside table. It was going on 7:15. She had plenty of time as she scheduled the "Chunnel" train, which left Waterloo Station, at 10:12. It would get her to Paris at 1:53, in the afternoon. Right now she would devote herself to breakfast and the news of the day.

She sat down, poured herself a cup of coffee and began leafing through the paper. It was the usual array of political bashing, reports of official scandal, misfeasance, nonfeasance and malfeasance, with the occasional murder which seemed to be getting more frequent and heinous, as time went on; an alarming trend, she thought to herself.

A small article, not much larger than a notice, caught her eye. "American geneticist teams up with ex-Cambridge professor." It went on to give a brief summary of the work to be conducted at the Foundation, naming Dr. Joanna Russo as an associate. Of course, this was nothing but a clever ploy by Slattery to validate the Foundation by controlling information to the public and further internationalizing its profile by announcing that the American, Dr. Russo, had come aboard. This was certain to displease her friend. But, considering what was at stake, she was certain that she could trust Jo's good sense not to react, to it, one way or the other. Fiona finished up with her breakfast, dressed and called down to the desk to arrange foe a cab to be waiting when she checked out.

After going through formalities at the desk, she was in the taxi and on her way to the second leg of her journey, the train to Paris. At that hour of the day the traffic was abominable. Finally, she arrived at the station, boarded the train, stowed her meager luggage and settled back in her seat for the journey under the Channel and on to France. Jo was on her mind. She knew that her friend was intelligent and resourceful, but, under these uncertain circumstances, she was uncomfortable about leaving her, even for this short period of time. But, the trip was a necessity even though the outcome, as to what would be discovered, was uncertain.

The noise of the train faded into the background and was unnoticeable to her as were her fellow passengers. Her only awareness was her thoughts as the train sped to its destination. All of the questions about Slattery and the Foundation kept returning. And what of Saint −Nazaire?

What part did Slattery's enigmatic trip play in the plot, as a whole? Was this a wild goose chase? Did the truth lie elsewhere? St-Nazaire was in and of itself a unique place. It came into its own in the nineteenth century, as a large modern port, even serving a stint as a center for U-Boat operations in WWII, when ships became to large to sail up the Loire to Nantes, the original and ancient harbor and center of commerce for that area. Perhaps, she considered, Nantes was the place to go to begin to unravel the mystery in which she and her friend found themselves and which may, very well, have cost Peter his life. The matter of Peter's death was of growing concern to her. She didn't believe Slattery, even though driven by ambition, to be capable of violence. The same, however, could not be said for those with whom he now associated himself. Of that she was absolutely sure. What was of particular annoyance and somewhat disconcerting was that although there was, clearly, some level of danger, it did not present itself in such a way so as to be confronted in a direct way. The only course of action available, at least for the present was to be alert while moving forward towards a solution. They would have to count on Slattery and company being heavily involved in their own tasks and finding it necessary to be as low key as possible to prevent bringing unwanted attention to themselves as some assurance that they would not resort to violence or, at least any further violence, if one could attribute Peter's death to them. This would be especially applicable to Jo who now had a measure of protection by being a much publicized associate of Slattery.

CHAPTER THIRTEEN

The train had reached its destination and pulled into Paris Nord. Fiona had her work cut out for her and there was no time to lose. She gathered up her luggage and set out to pick up a car. The Jag was too conspicuous. It would be a two hundred mile trip from Paris through the French countryside of the Pays de la Loire to her final destination of Nantes. She knew that she would arrive too late this day to accomplish anything. Her search for answers would begin tomorrow.

CHAPTER FOURTEEN

Jo's day, at the Foundation, was ending. It had been a tediously long and unfruitful Tuesday. She harbored a strong feeling of failure for having spent so much time at the lab without coming up with something, anything. It was obvious to her that simply being there, in and of itself, was not going to offer up any revelations as Peter had hoped. Everything looked innocuous. The activities being carried on were well cloaked and compartmentalized. Time was not on her side and somehow she had to break through the barrier that protected the true nature of Slattery's research. She reflected on Fiona and what she would find in Saint-Nazair. As she exited the lab, she remembered that she had no car and that it had been left at the flat to be picked up for repairs which, hopefully, had been completed. Piero, where was Piero? He was supposed to drive her back.

She heard the familiar roar of the engine and saw the bright yellow motorcycle coming quickly up the path towards the lab. It stopped directly in front of her, Piero revving the engine with one hand and handing her the spare helmet with the other. No words, not even a greeting were exchanged between the two. They roared off down the path, the cycle kicking up dirt and pebbles as they sped through the entry way, going ever faster as they passed through the gate and as Piero expertly guided the machine down the road and finally on to the main thoroughfare. He had turned in the direction opposite of the route which took them back to Cambridge. Jo patted him on the back, extended her arm in front of him, motioning with her thumb to go the other way. Waiving off her objection he continued on his way. The cycle accelerated and the landscape flashed by Jo's peripheral vision. She hung on to Piero, looking over his shoulder, giving her a clear view of the speedometer as the needle rapidly changed reading; 70-80-90-100, stopping its climb at 110 miles per hour. She had no feeling of fear or even anxiety but, rather, excitement. She was, for the moment, living on the edge, pushing the envelope of physical danger and savoring every glorious moment of it. Her grip on the young man tightened as the motorcycle seemingly flew down the road until, finally slowed down and made the turn into a parking lot adjoining a country pub. They dismounted the cycle and removed their helmets. Jo noticed Piero staring at her.

"Something wrong?", she asked.

"Your face, it's flushed. Your not frightened by speed, are you?"

"I hadn't experienced quite that much on the back of a motorcycle, before."

"And you found it?" Piero paused, waiting for her answer.

Jo thought for a second. "Exciting."

"Something new and something you'd like to experience again?"

"Yes. Yes, I suppose you could say that."

"It's an extraordinary day when one discovers something new about one's self", he observed.

"And you Piero, what about you?"

He said nothing in response, but, smiled and gestured for them to enter the pub.

It was one of those up market establishments that served cuisine rather than the usual pub fare and catered to the well heeled population of the region. It was also a place where, apparently, Piero was well known as could be deduced from the warm and familiar greeting directed to her companion from the young, attractive hostess. She seated them and inquired if they wished something to drink. Before Jo could respond, Piero ordered.

"A bottle of Mumm's, please. I trust that champagne will be suitable, Doctor?"

"Very suitable and were not at the Foundation, so Joanna will do just fine."

The hostess returned with the champagne, uncorked the bottle and proceeded to pour.

Piero raised his glass.

"What shall we drink to?", he asked Jo.

"I didn't know we were celebrating anything."

Piero looked at her, intensely, with a knowing gaze that seemed to penetrate her mind. "There are always moments to celebrate or things past to remember and those things which are yet to come, unfortunately such moments, too many times, are lost."

"Then, Piero, I'll leave it to you not to lose this one".

"Then let me toast to you and wish that you prevail in finding all that you seek."

An appropriate toast, she thought, more appropriate than her young companion could know or imagine. But, then again, perhaps not.

Piero's graciousness and the champagne put her at ease. The two engaged in some small talk which focused, generally, on her professional background. As the dining room filled up, it's surroundings became more comfortable, the low volume din of he other patrons, engrossed in their own conversations giving a sense of privacy to Jo as to the things said between her and Piero. They were only interrupted by the waitress taking their dinner order.

The talk then turned to matters of Piero, Slattery and the Foundation. Jo had never been satisfied with Slattery's explanation of Piero and how he came to be his ward. She did her best to pursue the subject as diplomatically as possible, extracting information as to what Piero knew about the compound. There was something enigmatic about him which was, perhaps, part of the answer to the Foundation.

Jo took a sip of her champagne, put her glass down and turned her full attention to her dinner companion.

"So, enough about me. Tell me something about yourself."

"What would you like to know?"

"Everything", Jo answered, with an engaging smile.

Piero leaned back in his chair and laughed.

"That may not be as much as you think."

"And what do I think?"

"You think; who is this man, where did he come from, why is he here, what does he do."

"Something like that."

"I'm sure you've already inquired about me to the Doctor."

"No. You came up in brief conversation, but, Dr. Slattery didn't reveal much except to say that you were born in China, you're parents died and eventually, the Doctor became your guardian and mentor."

"That is mostly all that I've been told about myself."

"And is that enough?"

"Whether it is or not, is not relevant and is something with which I don't concern myself. I know that I was raised in China, up to the point that Doctor Slattery took custody of me. But, I have no memory of my parents or what their fate may have been."

"Did Dr. Slattery ever offer to give you further details on your background?"

"No and I never asked him to. It's a topic which has never been breached, except in the most superficial way."

"And that's that?"

"Yes. As you put it, that's that. Dr. Slattery has offered me a good life in England. I come and go as I please and pursue my own interests."

"Which I presume are different from those of the Foundation?"

"Some times they intersect."

"And what are your interests. Piero?"

The conversation was interrupted by the waitress delivering their orders and Jo's question was left unanswered. She nibbled at her platter of excellent, grilled sole. Dinner was not on her mind. Piero, on the other hand, ate heartily. His personality, if not his personal history, was already revealing itself. Jo saw a young man who exhibited a keen and insightful mind, sometimes philosophical in nature. He embraced sensual pleasures; speed, good food and good wine in a way and with a depth that belied his youth. His appetite was not limited to inanimate objects. His informality with some of the female staff of the pub and their reaction to him, showed an appreciation of beautiful young women, an appreciation which was reciprocated.

Her evening with Piero was turning out to be much more than she expected and the evening had a long way to go.

He poured the rest of the champagne and placed the empty bottle upside down in the ice bucket to signal the waitress.

"Shall we order another bottle?", he asked.

"I don't think so. It's getting late and besides, I want you in shape to drive the motorcycle."

"We could enjoy the champagne elsewhere, at out leisure and there's no reason for you to go back to the flat. Your car was in the garage and that tells me your friend is out of town. Why go back to empty rooms?"

"And where would that elsewhere be?", queried Jo, with a smile.

"The proprietor of the pub allows me to rent one of the rooms upstairs. It's modest, but, it allows me needed solitude away from the compound."

"Am I being seduced?"

"I have a higher regard for you, than that. We have, however, been thrown together by fate for some purpose which is still unclear, to me. But, I believe, our relationship is a unique one and both of us should take advantage of whatever experiences we can share. It is unlikely that we will have another opportunity."

Jo nodded her head in the affirmative, but, said nothing. She sat there in silence reflecting on the occurrences of the last couple of weeks that all started with her decision to respond to, what appeared to be, an innocuous letter sent by a college professor from her past. Piero ordered the second bottle of champagne and took care of the check. The two then departed the dining room and took a back staircase to his apartment.

The quarters were comfortable and sparse. There were no books or, for that matter, any other publications; not even a magazine or newspaper. There was no computer, no television nor a radio. There was only a large sketching pad propped up against a chair in the corner of the room.

"Well, what do you think of my little hideaway?"

"It's very pleasant, but, it hardly looks like anyone lives here."

"I don't. I live at the compound and come here only when I need to get away."

"Is that often?"

"Often enough."

"But, what do you do here?"

"I see you've noticed that I have none of the usual amenities that one usually has in order to provide distraction. But, I don't find artificial distraction necessary. When I come here, I think. I find that my thoughts are more than enough to occupy me. For sustenance, I simply find my way downstairs."

Piero walked over to a night stand and rummaged through the drawer, pulling out a pencil and turned on the bedside lamp, making a slight adjustment to the shade.

"Joanna, come here and sit on the edge of the bed, near the light.'

She complied, not quite knowing what to expect.

The young man took her, gently, by the shoulders and positioned her so that the bedside lamp properly illuminated her face. "That's perfect. I hope you don't mind if I sketch you."

"Not at all."

"But first", exclaimed Piero as he popped the champagne cork, fetched two glasses from a shelf and poured. He raised his glass.

"To the moment."

"To the moment", Jo responded

Piero moved his chair closer to the bed and sat there, silently, for a moment, looking at Jo with a contemplative gaze. He raised the pad and began to sketch.

"Do I have to sit perfectly still?"

"No. You can move a bit. I'll compensate."

Jo took a sip of her champagne.

"Tell me Piero, do you have a good relationship with the Doctor?"

"How do you mean?"

"Do you like him?"

"I have respect for him; for his dedication. And you, what convinced you to come to the Foundation?"

"Professional curiosity, for the most part and maybe a need for change."

Have you found what you're looking for, professional satisfaction and change, that is?"

"I don't think I've had enough time to answer that?"

"And what about Dr. Slattery, do you like him?"

"I respect his dedication", she responded, with a note of sarcasm.

Piero looked at her with a smile.

"Look this way a bit", he requested as he continued sketching.

The conversation was no longer just small talk. They were verbally fencing. Words and phrases were like foils, first fending off an attack then probing and thrusting to get the advantage and expose a vulnerability. But, it was apparent that no one was going to shout *touché* tonight. It was just as well as Jo was thoroughly enjoying the night, the champagne and most of all, the company. She sensed a trust between them and each would have to decide how far that trust would go. It was certain that there would be more conversations about Slattery and the Foundation.

Nothing more was said, Jo sipping from her glass and Piero concentrating on the sketching of the portrait.

After a surprisingly short time, he stopped.

"May I see?"

"Not yet. It needs finishing. I'll let you see it when the time is right."

Piero went over to the closet and leaned the sketchpad in a corner. He turned and started to walk over to Jo who was still sitting on he edge of the bed. She was anticipating, but, still unsure what the rest of the night would bring.

CHAPTER FIFTEEN

Fiona woke early to greet her first day in Nantes, determined to make her arduous trip worth it. Her hunch was that because both Saint-Nazaire and Nantes were maritime centers, in the past as well as the present, investigation in these two cities would be the likeliest place to begin her initial line of inquiry. She took a moment to call the flat and leave a message for Jo, letting her know that she had arrived safely without revealing her destination on the message tape.

Nantes, a centuries old city in the Pays de la Loire, was one of those places filled with historical content. The Musee Jules Verne pays homage to the nineteenth century visionary who called Nantes home. Verne, like da Vinci, was a man whose ideas were far ahead of his time. Although presented as tales of adventure and fiction, much of what Verne wrote were in the nature of predictions of what would come to pass long after he, himself, was gone. Was Verne just a great storyteller with an incredibly fertile imagination, or, was there something more to it, she asked herself.

She strolled through the town looking for something or someplace to begin her search, her path taking her to the dry moat of the majestic Chateau de Nantes which was a good place to be only if you were interested in observing architecture or the locals walking their dogs. But, tourist attractions would not be the places where she would hope to find the information she needed to uncover. No, it would be the backstreets, less traveled and the places, more obscure, which would be the most probable to bear fruit.

Considering that the clues had led her to this place, all of her instincts were telling her that she was looking for something maritime. Something lost through the ages. She bypassed the museums and the more frequented curio shops. What she was looking for was something lost in time, without obvious importance or value, but, easily recognizable when found and something which would define the puzzle if not solve it.

Her investigation took her up and down every road and backstreet of Nantes. She was certain that this would be the place where, if there was something to be found, it would be found. Finally, at the end of a long, tiring and frustrating day, she came upon a small out-of-the-way shop bearing the sign, "ANTIQUITE, Carte Marine – Journal de Bord". Fiona's hopes were immediately elevated. The shop dealt in articles old and maritime. She scrutinized the contents on display in the window and was filled with anticipation that there would be something material which, upon exploration, the shop would yield up. The entry door of dark wood and etched glass was slightly ajar as if to beckon a passersby to enter. Fiona went in and quickly scanned the premises. It was, indeed, a fascinating place holding articles of every description, from small, odd pieces to nautical charts and instruments to pieces of furniture. One magnificent and ornate desk, which stood out above the rest, caught her eye. As she went over to more closely examine it, she was approached by the proprietor, a very attractive, thirtyish woman clad in a dark blue, well tailored suit with a friendly yet to-the-point manner. She was very professional while maintaining an aura of civility, culture and grace which enhanced the ambiance of the shop.

"Bon jour, Mademoiselle."

"Bon jour."

"May I be of assistance, to you?", the woman inquired, with only the slightest trace of a French accent.

"Yes, I'm looking for anything that you might have in the nature of logs or records dating back to the early 1500's." Fiona set the date of inquiry to correspond with Jo's da Vinci theory.

"Please come this way", the woman responded as she gestured for Fiona to follow her to a back area of the shop. There stood a set of tall, glass-doored book cabinets which contained a considerable number of leather bound volumes, being originals and reproductions of logs of many of the merchant ships that sailed from Nantes when it was the center of maritime activity in the region. Her knowledge was extensive and impressive and she was, clearly, more of a curator rather than, simply, a merchant of the artifacts contained in the shop. The logs and manuscripts were explained, in some detail, but, were of little interest to Fiona as she gave them a cursory review. This lack of enthusiasm as a reaction to the contents of the documents was sensed by the woman. She asked Fiona to accompany her to the shop's office.

"Come with me, I've something else to show you. It's not for sale, but, its background might be of some interest to you."

Fiona became aware that the woman had deduced that she was looking for information, not antiques and apparently, was willing to be accommodating. She led Fiona into the office and stopped next to what was, very obviously a large, extremely old, rough hewn desk.

"I don't understand", she stated.

The woman explained, "This desk is a symbol of a tale of events which happened centuries ago, during the period in which you expressed interest, be they true or simply a myth has not been established for a certainty. The desk, it is said, is fashioned from the timbers of a ship that was broken down after returning to Nantes, from a voyage, in the 1500's. It's last voyage, as the story goes, was to deliver an artifact or relic, of some sort, that came from a place near Amboise to a destination which remains, to this day, unknown. There was a ship's log kept, under lock, in the desk. It was, supposedly, the log of the ship that provided the timbers for the desk, itself. Although we retain the desk, the log, itself, went up for auction, some years ago and was sold to a Chinese gentleman for a substantial sum."

"Do you have any record of the contents of the log?"

"No. It was stipulated, as part of the auction, that no copies or records of any kind could be retained. The only record of what is written in the log, is the log itself. However, judging from the price paid, it had significant meaning to the party or parties who bid on it."

Fiona felt a sense of frustration and disappointment.

"Well, I thank you for your time and information."

"I don't know if you found what you were looking for, but, I hope that visit to our establishment has satisfied at least some of your curiosity and your reason for coming to Nantes.

"Yes. Yes it has. Merci"

"Fiona shook the woman's hand, turned and exited the shop onto the street with her one and only thought being to get back to Cambridge as soon as possible.

CHAPTER SIXTEEN

Sunrise came too quickly. Jo was filled with the grogginess that comes with a late night, followed by an early morning. She had to stop for a moment to collect her thoughts and counter the mild confusion of waking up to unfamiliar surroundings. She glanced around the room, but Piero seemed to have disappeared. His absence was short lived as he came through the door carrying a tray.

"The advantages of living over a restaurant with access to the kitchen", he announced, glancing down at the tray bearing two café au laits and a basket of rolls.

"I thought that you might need something to restore your energy after last night", he declared, smiling at Jo, as he set the tray on the night table, at the same time leaning over to give her a gentle kiss on the lips.

"I thought some coffee might be welcome", observed Piero as he handed Jo one of the cups.

"How about coffee and conversation. It seems we didn't do much talking last night".

"What would you like to talk about?"

"You."

"Just me?"

"Well, you and the Foundation."

"What would you like to know?"

"Everything."

Piero smiled.

"Everything may not be much. But then, it might be more than you want or are prepared to know."

"Which do you think it would be?"

"That would be for you to decide."

"Do you feel that telling me about yourself would be a betrayal of Dr. Slattery, or, that last night and now is a betrayal?"

"That might depend."

"On what?"

"On your motivation for asking the questions; or, on who you are."

Jo paused to assess her companion. They both sat silently, each contemplating the other. It was at that moment that she deduced that Piero was not only the bright and introspective young man that she had always thought him to be. He was, she concluded, much more.

"Do you feel a loyalty to the Doctor?". Asked Jo.

"What do you define as loyalty?"

"A self imposed duty never to act against his interests, no matter what they may be."

"That would be blind and absolute loyalty and no person owes that to any other person. There are always equities to be considered and judgments to be made. I consider myself to be associated with Dr. Slattery. He doesn't own me nor does he have a right to expect me to whimsically or foolishly submit my will to him on his demand. That has never been our relationship nor will it ever be."

"You sound so definite about that, but, doesn't it trouble you that you don't know who you are, that your only memory is of Dr. Slattery and not your parents?"

"My pedigree is not of particular importance to me and as for my memory, only I, shall we say, have knowledge of what I know and for another to draw conclusions as to that would be presumptuous. I don't wish to sound cold and matter of fact, but, you and I have reached a point where, for a number of reasons, some of which will become clearer to you in the near future, you should know something of who and what I am, at least as that may concern the relationship that we have and how that may affect other and larger matters."

He was right, she thought, it did sound cold. But, it was honest, almost to a fault. Although he was blunt, even challenging, she felt assured by his words. His response, both the words and their delivery, betrayed the fact that something was weighing heavily on him; something which he did not yet want to divulge.

Jo pressed on. "Do you feel that the Dr. would approve of us and the last twenty four hours which we spent together?"

"Dr. Slattery has never imposed upon me either his approval or disapproval in what I do. In that limited respect we are compatible."

"Do you approve of what he is doing at the Foundation? Do you even know what the purpose of the Foundation is?"

"Yes. But, it isn't something that I can divulge right now. That will come in time. As for what my judgment is of him, it is the same relationship as him with me. It is not couched in terms of approval or disapproval. I have simply concluded that the Dr. does not truly understand the implications or the depth of where his research is taking him."

Jo wasn't sure what to make of the young man's cryptic answer.

"What do you mean?"

"Let me say that Dr. Slattery, brilliant as he is, is flawed by a limited and materialistic view of the potential outcome and underlying consequences of the research in which he's involved. There's no doubt that this is caused, in large part, by the nature of those individuals he calls his colleagues and who are his benefactors. These are people of power and wealth, with little or no vision, whose only desire is to increase that power and wealth, exponentially."

Jo felt excitement that she was at a breakthrough point in her search for details on the Foundation and was eager to press forward in her conversation with Piero. But, it was not to be, at least not here, not now. He interrupted, pointing out that it was getting late and he had to drive her back to the flat so she could change and pick up the

Mini which, hopefully, had been repaired and returned by the rental agency. The conversation had changed Piero's mood. He seemed intense and troubled, something she hadn't seen in him before. He had a lot to tell and she hoped that she would provide the outlet for his story. Where else could he turn? He was raised in China under mysterious circumstances and brought to England as the ward of a man who, himself was not independent of those who had controlled Piero for the early part of his life. Although he had some superficial freedom from the control of others, he was, in fact, isolated. For whatever reason, he had chosen Jo as his means to strike out against his insular existence.

She rode the motorcycle back to the flat. The trip was quiet and surreal. She was so deep in contemplation of her night and morning spent with Piero, as to both their physical and intellectual intimacy that she hardly heard the noise of the engine or felt the wind against her face. It seemed that no time at all had passed and they were making their way down the side street which led to the flat. She was relieved to see the Mini parked out front. She and Piero said very brief goodbyes and Jo raced up the stairs to get herself dressed and organized for work. She entered the apartment and hastened over to the blinking light of the message machine and pressed the "play" button. It was Fiona. Her welcome voice simply said that she had reached her destination safely. There was nothing more. It was apparent that there would be no further messages and she would not know the outcome of her friend's trip until she returned to Cambridge. Right now the important thing was to get to the compound and continue her work their. She pondered her relationship with Piero and the events of the past twenty four hours. She felt, in her bones, that, in some unexplained way, he was the keeper of the knowledge of the essential truth of the Foundation.

CHAPTER SEVENTEEN

After a fitful night's sleep, Fiona began the journey that would take her back to Cambridge. Her findings in Nantes, although not tangible, were certainly material. Whoever had come to secure possession of the log did not do it randomly or speculatively. They knew of Nantes and Saint-Nazaire and the significance of these places. They knew what they were looking for and spent a great amount of effort and funds to acquire it. She was convinced that the person or persons who purchased the log were not simply collectors of maritime antiquities and that her thinking was correct in concluding that the reason for possessing it was not for the purpose of obtaining historical information or for some noble scientific purpose but, rather, to assure that the log and its contents did not fall into unfriendly hands. The one reassuring aspect to her trip was that she could be confident that the Foundation wouldn't have bothered to tail her to the continent, even if they knew that she was government and what her motivation was for going there. They would know that nothing could or would be found. Nantes and Saint-Nazaire would no longer have any importance to those with whom Slattery was involved. The log was gone, either destroyed or held, somewhere, under the tightest security and gone with it were any secrets it may have held. But, for those who took it, it would be a miscalculation on their part to believe that the trail would be left so cold that any further endeavor by those in pursuit of the truth would be futile. The fact was, that although an important clue was gone, its very removal provided a piece to the puzzle, no matter how small or seemingly insignificant.

The countryside was just a blur and Fiona had all she could do to concentrate on the road as she sped back to Paris. As she put her thoughts together on her experiences in Nantes, everything seemed to be a paradox. She thought of the old theorem, unproven though it might be, that if man or woman can imagine something, it is possible or, conversely, man or woman cannot imagine something that is impossible. Then, is imagination really imagination or is it a manifestation of something much more. The greatest history's writers of fiction predicted things that were to happen long after they had passed from this world. Did they possess fertile imaginations or perhaps, in some way, give us a glimpse, not of the possible or even the probable, but, of what, given sufficient passage of time, would be certain to happen. Fortune telling, of a sort, but, not of a supernatural or mystical quality, rather, pre-programmed intellect of everything known or to be known by humankind, but, designed to reveal itself sequentially, in logical phases. But, throughout recorded history, there have been those who revealed bits and pieces of that knowledge out of continuity and time. *Could it be that Slattery and the Foundation have something which would allow them to accelerate human knowledge drastically, yet in an orderly and usable way?* Then she thought as to whether her own thoughts were a nexus to the unproven theorem. *Did the fact that she derived this deduction, from the storehouse of her own intellect, make it a reality or was it all just her imagination?* The thought was, at the same time intriguing and in its own way, amusing.

She turned her full concentration to her driving and pressed on the accelerator. There was no time to waste. She picked up her cell phone from the passenger seat and called the flat. Perhaps she could catch Jo. No luck. She left a simple message that she was on her way back

CHAPTER EIGHTEEN

Jo raced along in the Mini. It was still early, but, she was anxious to get to the compound. The now familiar drive was filled with monotony broken only by the thoughts racing around in her mind. Was the night spent with Piero merely a spontaneous happening, or not? Was the Mini intentionally disabled to give him a chance to establish a closer relationship outside the influence of the Foundation. Their short time together did give her some additional insight into the young man but, as with other leads, answers led to more questions. She was eager to find out what Fiona had learned on her trip to the continent. She was also cognizant of the fact that as things progressed and the web became more intricate, the danger to the both of them would increase. Piero was an insider and even though he expressed independence from Slattery, she couldn't be sure how far she could actually trust him.

The route to the compound had become almost instinctive and her turnoff from the main highway to the side road was automatic. Before she knew it she was, once again, at the main gate. The monotony of the routine was broken by the sound of Piero's voice emitting from the call box. There were, however, no pleasantries exchanged as their relationship had to remain guarded and besides, she did not fully trust the young man. The gate opened and she proceeded through with a feeling of annoyance that she did not have free access to the compound. This reinforced her belief that her relationship with Slattery remained tentative. There was an underlying conflict. How deep it ran and how much of a danger it posed was an unknown quantity. Perhaps she would have to abandon her plan to curry favor with Slattery in her role as a fellow scientist and take more direct and risky action in order to discover the answers that she was looking for; the answers that she had to find.

She drove down the path toward the building housing her assigned lab. As she passed the building which she dubbed the "bunker", a feeling of excitement rushed through her. The door, it had not been completely closed. Again, this had to be the result of the absent mindedness of Jack. It was a stroke of unbelievable luck tempered by the realization that if the door was ajar, Jack was probably inside and would be leaving within a short period of time. Her anticipation was mixed with anxiety as she pulled the Mini into its parking space next to her lab building. She got out and began slowly walking toward the open door while making every effort to maintain her composure and to not be obvious. After a few moments, she found herself at the entrance. Although she had some trepidation, it was something that she had to do. This morning she was full of questions and uncertainty. Now, she was on the threshold of what might very well be the portal to the answers.

Her eyes darted around as she walked through the entrance, trying to take in as much detail of the structure as she could, as quickly as she could.. The main entry door appeared to be solid metal, probably steel, possibly titanium for maximum security, approximately four inches thick with an electronic locking device which, it seemed, when triggered deployed a series of one inch thick bolts into the reinforced frame . She took hold of the edge and swung it slightly, back and forth. She was surprised at the ease with which it moved. There was no sensation of weight, at all, due, no doubt, to a specially engineered hinge system. The entry way, just inside the door looked to be about eight feet high and six feet in both width and depth. After she entered the main room, she knocked on the interior wall. Solid concrete. The depth of the entry way no doubt disclosed the thickness of the exterior walls of the building. The building was, in fact, exactly what it looked like. It was a bunker, blast proof and virtually impenetrable. But, what was so precious that such extraordinary protective measures had to be taken? She didn't have long to ponder as she heard the sound of an electric motor. Her attention was drawn to a squared off structure protruding from the rear wall which contained a metal door and a security panel to the right, similar to the one next to the exterior door of the building. Otherwise, the inside of the building was just a large empty, inhospitable space painted light gray and dimly lit by fixtures recessed in the ceiling. Whatever work was done here and whatever treasure was kept on these premises, it was underground.

She concluded that the electric motor she heard was operating an elevator and that the door located at the far wall would, shortly, be sliding open to reveal its occupant who, no doubt, would be Jack. She had only seconds to make her choice as to whether to retreat or remain. Such option, however, was taken from her when she heard the voice of Slattery, behind her.

"Good morning Joanna."

As she turned to face Slattery, the noise of the electric motor stopped and the door slid open. She had guessed correctly. Out of the corner of her eye, she could see Jack emerge. A feeling of alarm swept over her, but, she knew that to act flustered or alarmed would be the wrong and possibly, the dangerous thing to do. Her body language and the tone of her voice exuded confidence and control. She was getting pretty damned good at this, she thought to herself.

"Good morning Doctor"

"I see that you've decided to do a bit of exploring."

Slattery was polite, but, she could detect the underlying annoyance and sarcasm in his greeting."

"I was on my way to the lab and I noticed the outside door to this building was open."

"And curiosity got the best of you."

"Yes, I suppose you could put it that way. Professional curiosity, that is. And I'm not aware of any restriction to my accessing any of the facilities in the compound."

"No, no. Of course there are no restrictions", Slattery assured her in an awkward and hesitating manner.

Slattery looked past her at Jack who, she sensed, was standing very close behind her waiting for his master's command. The Doctor was glaring at him with great dissatisfaction, no doubt for his continued carelessness in failing to secure the door to the bunker.

"Dr. Russo and I have matters to discuss. Go back and take care of things at the house."

Jack proceeded to leave, but, gave Jo a menacing glance as he passed her. She felt that she could handle Slattery. Jack was another matter. She never trusted his loyalty to the Doctor and consequently never believed that he had full control over him. It crossed her mind that Jack was there not to serve Slattery, but, to keep an eye on him and all that he did, including his association with former students.

As he left, Jack secured the door and Slattery turned his attention back to Jo.

"I would have brought you here in due course, but, now that you've moved the process ahead, come with me."

Slattery led her to the elevator. They stepped into what turned out to be an elevator of considerable size, obviously designed to carry freight, probably some sort of lab equipment, as well as people. They descended rapidly and Jo's stomach felt very much the same as the sensation she got when riding high speed elevators in New York. It took only a few seconds to reach the bottom. She guessed that they were somewhere in the neighborhood of fifty feet below ground. If her calculations were correct and taking into account the structure of the building, this would make it virtually impenetrable except by the use of extraordinary means. The door opened and Slattery gestured with his arm for Jo to exit the elevator.

"This way Joanna."

She followed him as she surveyed her surroundings. The area in which she found herself was in keeping with what one might expect given the outer appearance of the building. The walls were of concrete, unfinished except for a coating of muted white paint, likewise the floor. An array of bright, florescent lights covered the ceiling. The one thing that was notable was that the area was not set up for any activity to be carried on. There was no laboratory equipment at all. The whole building was nothing but a vault built for the protection of whatever was being kept there. Although she couldn't see them, she was sure that there were other security devices on the premises, listening and watching. At the center of the room was a large cylindrical object which was not sitting on the floor, but, actually built into it. She recognized it as a cryogenic chamber, although quite a bit larger than then ones she was accustomed to seeing in her work. It also had the same type of palm or finger print identification panel that secured the outer door to the building. Slattery walked over to the device and turned towards Jo.

"What you see before you, Joanna, contains the heart and soul of the work at the Foundation. It's just as well that I present you with the facts now so that we can get on with the research that you are here to conduct."

"Then everything up till now has been a charade?", Jo retorted.

"No, not a charade, rather, a precaution."

She watched as Slattery placed his hand on the security panel which gave off a faint green glow. There were a series of beeps indicating that the mechanism had been activated followed by the dull metallic sound of the chamber being unlocked. There was the low hum of hydraulics as the thick, heavy lid slowly rose allowing the white mist caused by the sub zero temperatures created by liquid nitrogen to escape into the air. Slattery then stepped over to a console a few feet from the chamber which contained some controls as well as a computer and screen. She watched intently as he began operating the controls. Perhaps, what she learned by observation would serve her well in the immediate future.

She maintained a calm exterior, but, she could feel the adrenalin rush as she stood there witnessing a scene which reminded her, with some amusement, of a B science fiction movie out of the 50's. Upon the lid opening to a ninety degree angle, Slattery flipped a switch on the panel and what appeared to be a rack, containing rows of small metallic containers, emerged from its place of safekeeping.

"These", Slattery proudly emoted," represent the central work of the Foundation."

"Embryos?"

"Not quite."

At that moment in time the veil of civility and gregariousness, which Slattery hid behind, parted and revealed the ego and ambition that she had not seen before in the man who had been a mentor in simpler days.

"These cylinders contain daughter cells", continued Slattery, "but, of a most unique nature. Let me show you."

He pressed some keys on the computer. A virtual representation of a DNA molecule appeared on the screen.

"Take a look and tell me what you see."

Jo directed her attention to the screen with the expectation tat she would be looking at something that she had seen thousands of times before in her work as a geneticist. But, as she studied the image she became aware that what the Doctor was presenting to her was something that was not part of her experience as a scientist.

"A DNA molecule", she remarked.

"Obviously", Slattery responded.

"But different."

"Yes".

"At first glance it seems usual and that the introns have been excised and that the coding patterns have been spliced together."

"But", coaxed Slattery.

"But, that's not the case."

"What do your eyes and expertise tell you, Dr. Russo?"

"There hasn't been a splicing. It appears that the introns have been replaced with additional coding sequences."

"Excellent", exclaimed Slattery. "I knew I chose well when I asked you to join me. Your observations are impeccable and your conclusions are totally consistent with scientific logic, but, there is something more. Take another look and let your mind reach a bit."

She continued to study the image of the molecule as Slattery stood by, eagerly awaiting the findings of her observations and in a way, once again becoming her teacher.

"It must be that the coding sequences were not spliced in; that they existed in the original DNA", she concluded.

"Exactly. Well done."

"Where did the DNA come from?"

"A fair question. Let me say, for now, that it came from a most unique source."

"From an original embryo?"

"No and that is part of the uniqueness. The source is, shall we say, of an exceptionally mature age, but, that does not seem to be an impediment to its being grown in a culture."

"Then, your cloning these cells. To what end?"

"More than that, Joanna, much more. We're at the frontier of unlocking genetic information which could advance human development in a way that would make everything that humanity has done, scientifically, to date, analogous to prehistoric man leaving his cave and looking in wonder at the sky, trying to understand the heavens and the nature of his own existence.."

Slattery's voice was excited and his eyes had an intensity that she had never seen before. She harkened back to Fiona's words the day they were having lunch just after she arrived in Cambridge. Now she saw it. There was a madness about Slattery. She was fascinated by the image of the DNA molecule and although she was now beginning to understand the nature of the Foundation and its work, it disturbed her that she was developing a fascination and a scientific curiosity probably of the nature which likely started Slattery down the path to what had become a dangerous and obsessive ambition.

The Doctor's voice seemed distant as she stood there occupied by her own thoughts, mentally processing what this all might mean and finally turning her attention back to Slattery as he continued his monologue.

"Our research addresses the coding or instruction to the DNA and the function of what I call the active introns and the possible effect on the ninety percent of DNA sequences the function of which is presently unknown."

"Have you come to any conclusions or, for that matter, developed any theories?"

"Only the possibility of a fifth and unknown nucleotide which triggers the proteins."

"Trigger them to do what?"

"Our hypothesis is that the activation of the coding sequences stimulate, in some way, those portions of the brain the function or purposes of which remain shrouded."

"Then you're speaking of a manner of evolutionary process?"

"Of a sort, but, not the Darwinian model of the straight line from simple to complex. You're, of course, familiar with experiments that were done on the eyes of Drosophilia, the common fruit fly."

"Yes. It was an unremarkable study in which eyeless fruit flies were bred and after a certain number of generations, of the strain, eyes reappeared. The experiment was interesting, but, more of a curiosity as opposed to any significant discovery which could be applied to mainstream research."

"Ah! You're reasoning like a member of the scientific establishment. Expand your thinking into the realm of imagination. What was your personal impression of that experiment?"

"That it was caused by some sort of corrective mutation."

"That is fine as far as it goes, but, you fail to take the additional steps down that path to the, shall we say corner, which you must turn in order to carry your deductions forward. It is or was more than merely some sort of correction to the way the fly's DNA is programmed. That route would take us to something that could result in a random outcome; something which might or might not happen. No, that cannot be the answer. What has taken place is that a mechanism was triggered to make the fly what it was; what it should be. That which had been was lost and then recaptured through the plan programmed in its genetic code, which wasn't lost at all, but, which was rendered dormant and somehow reactivated at a level and in a way not understood."

Slattery's words, from the past, echoed in her mind, *advancement then regression, knowledge found and lost. Was he suggesting that human intellect was at the stage represented by the blind fly and that the Foundation was on the brink of finding the genetic mechanism to replace those eyes or, rather human intellectual capacity or genetic memory which had, for some reason, been lost ages ago?* The question of the ethics of cloning seemed almost irrelevant compared with the magnitude and impact of such research. The implications of what Slattery had said was that the DNA molecule that they had obtained, from an undisclosed source, could in some way recreate, in humans, a faculty of limitless intellectual capacity or innate memory, previously possessed by ancient humans or even, possibly, some other predecessor going back to the remote and darkest reaches of time and space. The revelation brought her to the stark realization that whatever it was the she had become involved in was well worth killing for. The facts surrounding Peter's death and the potential risk to both her and Fiona would need serious reassessment. There could be no doubt, as far as she was concerned, that both of them were in imminent danger. For now, she had no choice but to continue her dialogue with Slattery and play along. It not only was necessary to the task at hand, but also, the best way to stay alive.

"Why the pretext in getting me over here to Cambridge?"

"Obviously, we certainly couldn't declare our real reasons in an open communication although it remains our position that what we are doing is legal, internationally and locally. Much of the world has a different perspective on human DNA research, such as this, than does the United States."

Jo disagreed with Slattery's observation on world opinion which was his rationalization for conducting research which, no doubt, went well beyond what he was willing to disclose to her.

"And what makes you think that I would consent to engaging in this line of experimentation?"

"Because you're a scientist and the Foundation is moving towards something which will dwarf anything that has gone before it in our discipline."

"That's quite an ambition."

"More than an ambition, Joanna; a goal which we are in the process of realizing."

"Then I can assume that those involved with you are equally determined."

"They are more than determined. They will let nothing stand in their way."

"That sounds like a threat."

"Come, come, Joanna, you know me better than that or, at least, I hope you do."

She turned away from Slattery back toward the computer screen without responding. It wasn't so much that she didn't believe the sincerity of his assurances as it was that, in his blindness, he had associated himself with people, the depth of whose ruthlessness, he didn't fully comprehend. He was a scientist who, for the most of his life, led a cloistered existence within the walls of an academic institution and now found himself in league with those who knew no bounds in an attempt to get what they wanted. In a way she felt sorry for him, but, knew that the madness had to be stopped in spite of the palpable risk to both her and her friend. The same danger applied to Slattery, if he decided not to do their bidding or waffled in any way on his commitment to carry forward with the Foundation's work. Regardless of the respect that she held for her former professor and the past that they shared, she had to come to terms that he was simply a pawn to be used by her in accomplishing her mission. The disturbing but undeniable thought crossed her mind. He was expendable.

"I think we've done enough down here, for the time being", he stated, breaking the silence. "I'll close down and meet you back at the lab."

Jo proceeded to exit the area while visually searching the premises to detect, if possible, any weakness that could be exploited in order to re-enter the building and access the cryogenic vault. The task seemed daunting. She left the building and made her way over to her car to gather up her briefcase. Upon opening the door leaning in to retrieve it from the passenger seat where she had left it, she found that it had been moved to the floor. She opened it, hurriedly checking the contents and discovered that, in addition to her personal papers and notes, it now contained a additional few pages, stapled together, which appeared to be copies. The cover page bore the title, "The Serpentine Foundation, Status Report on Fetal Development". Her mind flashed back to the red file given to Jack and the pregnant, Asian woman who was brought to the compound and who now resides in one of the secure brick buildings. But, how did the papers find their way into her briefcase? She looked over at the spot where she had noticed Piero's motorcycle parked when she came in earlier that morning. It was gone. Every instinct told her that the young man that she had come to know had become something more than she expected. In fact, she didn't know him at all.

CHAPTER NINETEEN

Fiona arrived back in Paris but was frustrated in her attempt to organize a return trip to London that day. Her concern about her friend grew. The matter of Peter's death had never been truly reconciled in her mind. She could not be sure if it was a hit and run accident or if in fact Peter was murdered. She knew that the same question haunted Jo although both remained silent on the possibility. They were dealing with ruthless people and as facts unfolded it was apparent that the stakes were, indeed, mush higher than either of them could have ever anticipated. She knew that she was in jeopardy and if Peter's death was Foundation connected, which was a likelihood, then she was the next logical target. Jo would be safe, for the immediate future, because of her association with the Foundation, which Slattery had made public. It was possible, she speculated, that the Doctor was more aware of his precarious position and the nature of those with who he had associated than she and Jo had given him credit got and going public with her name provided a layer of protection, no matter how thin. It was a comforting thought, but, not one that she could rely on. No one was indispensable to the Foundation and those that got in their way would be eliminated. Of that she had no doubt. For the next twenty four hours there was nothing that she could do except to tend to her own security and trust that Jo was resourceful enough to do the same for herself.

There was one discomforting thought that played on her mind. It was the woman at the shop who provided her with the information. If those who bought the logs had limitless funds and were willing to undertake extraordinary means to guard against those who would thwart their ambitions, it was not outside the realm of possibility that she may have been bought off as an informant to advise them of anyone who turned up asking the wrong questions.

Fiona returned to her hotel where she had kept her room during her visit to Nantes. So, unless she was being closely followed, it would appear, to anyone who inquired, that she had remained in Paris during the duration of her trip to the continent. She had also picked a hotel where a good old fashioned key was used and not one of those computerized entry cards which record your comings and goings.

"Bon jour", Fiona greeted the familiar face behind the reception desk as she entered the hotel lobby.

'Bon jour, Mademoiselle Clark", responded the clerk as he mentioned for her to come over.

"Do you have something for me?", she asked, curious in the fact that there should have been no message or phone call as not even Jo was aware as to the identity of the hotel in which she was staying.

"Nothing, except to let you know that there was an Asian gentleman asking about you, yesterday."

"And?"

"And, we advised him that we did not give out any information on our guests and that is our practice unless a guest indicates that we do otherwise."

"Did he come back?"

"No, although he was visibly displeased with my response to his inquiry."

"Merci."

"Not at all Mademoiselle, it is our pleasure."

There is little doubt that she was a focus of Slattery's colleagues. The question was, why. For now she would act on the premise that the Foundation's interest in her was generated by her association with Jo. It was a stroke of good luck that whoever was sent to track her was not much of a bloodhound and was unable to follow the scent beyond Paris. Nevertheless, she had an ominous sense that things were beginning to close in and that precious time was growing short.

CHAPTER TWENTY

Jo had completed another day at the Foundation. She had kept her briefcase, containing the files, close and had spent more of her energies keeping an eye on it then she did on her various assigned tasks at the lab. Finally, she found herself existing the compound on her way back to the flat. She had scanned the grounds before she left and Piero's motorcycle was nowhere to be seen. She was also concerned about Fiona and was anxious for her to return safely and to relate what, if anything, she may have discovered. Right now, her immediate plan was to find some solitude and to review the file which had found its way into her possession. She was especially vigilant on the road and wary of anything which might indicate that she was being followed. Her wariness had become more acute. The planting of the file was surely an indication that events had taken a turn; a turn which was favorable but which increased the dangers to those involved.

Jo drove into Cambridge that now represented, to her, a safe and comforting haven from the Foundation which was giving her the creeps. She wound her way through a couple of back streets and parked her car in the extra space in front of the apartment building. As she exited the Mini she looked up and down the street. There was no unusual activity as far as she could see. She walked up the stairs and let herself into the flat. As she closed the door behind her, she noticed that the light on the answering machine was blinking, showing a single message. She pressed the PLAY button and heard the welcome voice of Fiona.

"Jo, it's Fiona. Be back tomorrow."

That was all, but, it was enough. Now, it was time to examine the file.

At first glance the documentation seemed fairly unremarkable, but, upon close examination, Jo found certain points of interest. The paperwork consisted of the medical files of two female individuals and recorded the in vitro fertilization of both. No doubt, she thought, these were the two Asian women that she saw exit the Rover at the compound. There were, however, no names. Each of the subjects was identified by a code number. The records consisted of progress charts as to the fetus and general health reports as to the women, themselves. Apparently, according to the information, the original procedures were done at the Foundation and the women sent to Hong Kong for the gestation period. Apparently, the women had been returned to England to give birth. It was, probably, the hand of one of these patients exiting the building that she saw that day while she was observing the compound from the road overlooking he premises. That made sense.

As Jo continued to leaf through the pages, she came upon a handwritten section that was not consistent with the rest of the file. It seemed to be a part of a separate memo, possibly a diary entry. From her familiarity with his handwriting, she identified it as having been penned by Slattery.

"My visit here has served its purpose and is coming to its conclusion. Further development of the project will, by agreement of all parties, be conducted in England. This will provide the necessary control that I have insisted upon and also, some element of security as those with whom I find myself associating will stop at nothing to accomplish their end.

I have also made arrangements to take the Caucasian boy back to Cambridge, with me. They have lost interest in him. Residence in England will allow him to develop whatever potential he has. He is an enigma, but, I suspect that..."

The page ended, interrupting whatever further thoughts Slattery may have had. She did learn that the doctor was not as naïve as she had suspected. In spite of his seemingly blind ambition, he was quite aware of the dangers that lurked around him.

This didn't put him on her side, but, it gave them a certain commonality which could be exploited. Apparently, this entry was from a personal log much too important to be left behind as were the other personal papers abandoned to the closet at Cambridge. As to the source of the page, there could be little doubt. Only Piero would have access to the personal effects of Slattery. The scrap of text provided to her was not only helpful in providing a degree of insight into the Doctor, but, also a scant but tantalizing glimpse into the nature of her young friend. And what of Piero? She had not seen him all day, although he was about, at the Foundation, as evidenced by the file slipped into her briefcase. Her possession of the file meant that Piero had deduced that she was at the Foundation for reasons other than assisting Slattery. For now, he was only willing to dole out bits and pieces; information which he probably felt should be known simply because of her association with the Foundation. By his acts of cooperation he was declaring an alliance with her. However, his motivation was unclear. *What was in it for him? That was the obvious question. But, was it the right one?*

Jo took her attention from the file and walked over to the kitchen window which was located at the front of the flat, facing out to the narrow and usually quiet residential street leading up to the apartment building. She was gazing out into the darkness when headlights, coming around the curve in the road, caught her attention. The vehicle was traveling at an unusually slow speed as it rounded the bend. Something didn't seem right. She switched off the overhead light and continued to watch as the lights made their way down the street. Her body was high on adrenalin, but, it wasn't fear or even anxiety that she was feeling. Her mind was working furiously as it does in such situations in processing information and determining options. She watched intently as the car became visible. It was some sort of medium size, dark colored coupe which she didn't recognize. It slowed almost to a stop with its high beams illuminating her red Mini. It then continued into a U-turn, picked up speed and continued on its way, disappearing into the night.

"What in the hell was that all about?", was the question that immediately went through her mind. It wasn't the black Rover, but, that didn't provide much comfort. It was obvious that they, whoever they were, were looking for her or for Fiona, or, for both of them. What were they up to? Perhaps, there would be another accident. Maybe another hit and run. It could very well be that these were the people responsible for Peter's death, but, the bastards weren't going to get her or Fiona. She reached for the phone, but, thought the better of it. It was probably not a good idea to make a call. There was no telling if the flat was under electronic surveillance and anyway, there was nothing to say nor anything that could be done until Fiona got back to Cambridge. Her eyes scanned the living room which was illuminated by a single lamp. There was a small fireplace complete with the usual array of implements in a container next to it.. She walked over and grabbed the poker, turned off the light and sat in a chair located in a corner of the room next to the doors leading to the outside balcony. It seemed like a fairly strategic location should anyone attempt to enter the flat.. The quiet and the darkness was comforting and gave her some feeling of calm and security.

But there was the realization that she would have to be vigilant till the morning.

CHAPTER TWENTY-ONE

Jo was awakened by the first light of morning shining through the living room windows. She had dozed off, but, fortunately there were no other occurrences during the night. She sat here, still drowsy, trying to collect her thoughts and mentally reviewing the events of the previous day. Not everything was clear. What was clear was that she could not go back to the compound. If she did venture back, the chances are that she wouldn't get out alive. Slattery was also probably at risk but he was indispensable to them, at least for the time being. She was not. But, what was the next step to be? She needed some cold water on her face to fully wake up. As she was making her way to the bathroom, she heard the tone from the front door bell and someone knocking rather loudly. She stopped in her tracks, realizing that the poker, her faithful weapon that had been her companion all night, had been left on the floor next to the chair. She turned and walked, rapidly, back to the living room to retrieve it. In that short time, she was awash with thoughts reviewing who it was that might be on the other side of the door. *Was it someone form the compound, possibly Jack? Was it Piero? Had they come to kill her or abduct her? Would they come crashing through the door and shoot her where she stood?* She always marveled at how the human mind could instantaneously process separate bits of information in a critical situation. It was like thinking of everything simultaneously, but, being able, at the same time, to distinguish one bit from the other. With her trusty poker in hand, she addressed the entity standing outside.

"Who's there?"

"Courier, Dr. Russo," responded the female voice.

"Courier from where?"

"From Ms. Clark."

"I'm indisposed. Please leave it at the door."

"As you wish."

"I wish."

"Very well. But, please make sure that you read it immediately."

"I'll make a point of it."

Jo thought it odd that a courier would make such a request. She surmised that the courier was actually some sort of agent and that the message had something to do with the suspicious vehicle from last night. She went to the kitchen window and observed the young female, dressed in a typical uniform of black pants, white blouse and tie get into a small grey car and begin to drive away. About half way down the street, the car stopped and the young woman looked out the driver's side window up towards the front balcony of the flat. It seems that she wasn't going to leave until she was sure that Jo had taken possession of the envelope that she had delivered. Jo walked over to the door, squatted down and opened the door just enough so that she could reach the envelope. She waived it in the air allowing the courier to see that she had picked it up. The car then continued on its way.

Jo hurriedly ripped open the envelope, removing and unfolding the paper that it contained. It was from Fiona, as the courier had stated and contained a message which was short and to the point.

> "Jo, I'm on my way back and should arrive this evening. The flat is too dangerous for you to remain. Go to the desk. There is a key in the small, green urn. Unlock the bottom, left hand drawer. You'll find a pistol. Take it and the extra magazine of ammo. The gun is loaded but there's no bullet in the chamber. The safety is on. Leave it that way. Don't pack anything, you'll be conspicuous. Just take your briefcase with any relevant papers and the gun. Drive to the pub where Piero maintains his apartment and wait. Do not use your cell phone.
>
> Leave NOW!
> Fiona"

Jo was relieved to hear from her friend. She was anxious, but, not surprised that the situation had ratcheted up and that there was no question that they were all at risk. She was puzzled, however, at the choice of meeting place. It could only be that Piero, in some fashion had either deduced or learned of Fiona's role in this matter and had chosen to contact her and had chosen to keep it to himself. That bothered her on an emotional level even though, logically, it made sense. But, it was time to going.

She went to the desk and turned the small urn upside down. A key dropped out. She opened the desk drawer and saw the small, silver colored semi-automatic pistol. She found herself staring at the gun and reflecting how her seemingly innocuous trip to Cambridge to explore a career change had turned into a personal and life altering odyssey. As with many things she had experienced, recently, the realization was both frightening and exhilarating. As Fiona predicted, she wanted more of it.

She picked it up, carefully and examined it. The safety was on and there was a magazine in it. She took the gun and the extra ammunition magazine and put both in her briefcase along with some documents that she had gathered together including the file which had mysteriously appeared. She relocked the drawer and returned the key to the urn and turned on a few lights throughout the flat so that it would not look abandoned. Jo then hurriedly exited the flat pausing momentarily on the landing to survey the street. It was quiet and deserted with no pedestrian or vehicular traffic. She went over to the garage and made sure that it was locked so no one could check for the presence of a car or the absence thereof . Then, it was into the Mini and off to the pub to meet with Fiona and surely, Piero.

She would nave to be careful, but, because it was a weekday and she would be expected at the compound, chances are there would be nobody tracking her. Leaving the Cambridge city limits, she headed toward the less traveled country roads that led to the pub. The route was relatively free of traffic and felt safe. However, the gun in her briefcase spoke volumes as to the potential danger they now found themselves in.

Finally, the pub loomed ahead. As the hour was early, it was closed for business although there was some activity inside and a few cars, owned by the staff, parked outside. She looked for the familiar, yellow motorcycle. It was nowhere to be found. She continued to the back of the building when Piero suddenly appeared, waiving her to follow him and directing her to a large shed, which appeared to be an old carriage house, standing at the rear of the pub. The doors were open and Piero's motorcycle was inside. She pulled the Mini in, next to the cycle, took her briefcase and joined him as he closed the two large doors. Jo started to speak.

"Not now," interrupted Piero. "I'll explain everything, but, let's just get upstairs and out of sight."

As soon as they entered his rooms, Jo stopped at the entrance and turned toward him.

"What in hell is going on here?"

Without answering, Piero walked back to the door.

"Stay here."

"Is that an order?", Jo shot back at him in an impatient tone.

Piero turned around, walked over to her and took her hands in his.

"I'm sorry to be short, but, events are moving swiftly. I can't explain now, but, your friend will arrive here late today and I'll be back this afternoon. Meanwhile, if you need anything just go downstairs. The staff will take care of you."

"And Slattery?", queried Jo.

"It is what it is with the Doctor. Right now it will do no good to contact him."

Piero kissed her and walked out the door. Moments later she heard the sound of his motorcycle racing out of the parking lot and down the road. She stood there in the apartment, motionless, until the roar of the engine could no longer be heard and pondered what was in store for all of the players in this mysterious and sinister game.

CHAPTER TWENTY-TWO

The tension was growing and she was back to a diet of cigarettes and coffee which the staff of the pub graciously provided to her. Her time was occupied looking through the papers that she had brought with her, always uncomfortably conscious of the pistol which she kept secure in the briefcase. She hoped that nothing would occur, prior to Fiona's returning which would put her in a position of whether or not to use it.

As the hours passed, the combination of anxiety and boredom was almost intolerable. *Where was Fiona? Where was Piero? When in hell were they going to arrive?* She past the time away, in part, by reading the files of the two Asian women over and over again trying to extract something from the rather meager information that they contained. They were a clue, but, not an answer. Two women, probably two of many, fertilized at the compound, sent back to China during gestation and returned to the

Foundation to give birth. A procedure followed probably, in good part, at the insistence of Slattery to allow him to assert a large measure of control over the process yet minimizing the chances of discovery by authorities or other prying eyes of what was actually going on. She had come to realize that Piero was a large piece of the puzzle, perhaps more. There were times when she felt him to be in command of events and that he was merely playing a self imposed role of the dependant ward of Slattery. But, it was so subtle that the Doctor, in his obsession with his work, never picked up on it and gave the young man free and unsupervised reign beyond the watchful eyes of those who controlled the Foundation. He was becoming an ally. But, he remained an enigma. What was his motivation? This apartment, over the pub, had always mystified her. He was bright, extraordinarily so. He was well read and extremely perceptive. If he chose, he could dominate and control a conversation. He dabbled at art and was multilingual. Who knew what other knowledge, abilities and talents he possessed. Yet, his rooms were barren, devoid of books, papers or even the now ever present personal computer. There was nothing present which could be used to occupy or nurture an active mind. She walked over to the closet at the far end of the room where she recalled that Piero had stored the sketch that he had done of her. She felt awkward that she was about to violate his privacy, but, as she began to turn the knob, she stopped. She remembered that when Piero had stored the portrait, the closet looked to be empty, save for a few pieces of clothing hung from a rack. Whatever else might be in there and for whatever reason, would have to wait until Piero's return. It would be a breach of trust at a time when he was becoming ever more important player in uncovering the truth and was a large piece of the puzzle. Perhaps, she speculated, he was the puzzle, itself.

CHAPTER TWENTY-THREE

The morning and afternoon passed slowly. The boredom was excruciating and the only thing that kept her alert was the edginess she felt in speculating as to what the next hours would bring. It wasn't until late in the afternoon that she heard a car coming around the pub to the back lot. She looked out the window and saw the familiar Jaguar stop at the foot of the outside staircase which led up to the apartment. Jo rushed down as her friend exited the car and gave Fiona a long, welcoming hug.

"I thought you'd never get here. With all this stuff coming together I wasn't sure if you ran into a problem."

"No real problems, at least not yet. I got here as soon as I could. Apparently you got my message."

"It was a surprise. The knock on the door scared the hell out of me until I found out what was going on."

"There was no choice. You brought the pistol, didn't you?"

Yeah, it's in my briefcase."

"Good."

"Are you expecting that kind of trouble?"

"Maybe."

"Let's get your car out of sight."

Jo walked over to the shed and opened one of the large double doors, directing Fiona to pull in and park next to the Mini. Fiona emerged from the car and stopped, for a moment, looking up at the second floor apartment.

"So, this is the place", she remarked.

" This is it. Wait a second till I close up the shed."

"Do that. We don't want any prying eyes."

Fiona quickly surveyed the area for anything suspicious. For now, things seemed to be secure.

"Up the stairs", directed Jo.

As the two entered the apartment, Fiona stopped, turned around and checked the area, one more time.

They went in and Jo closed the door, behind them.

"Very clean, orderly and efficient, but, hardly a place to call home. No stuff", Fiona observed.

"That's the same reaction that I had about the place. I mentioned it to Piero, but, never really inquired about it", Jo commented.

"Why not?"

"I didn't think I'd get an answer."

"You mean he'd lie to you?"

"No. But, he has a way of giving you an answer without giving you an answer."

"Well, we're going to need some answers; a lot of answers. Where is Piero, now?"

"I don't know. I assume that he had some loose ends to tie up at the compound. I was sure that he'd be back now."

"His going back there wasn't a safe thing to do."

"Well, he's pretty resourceful and I think he knows what he's doing."

"Just the same, I hope he gets back soon. I think things are falling apart at the Foundation."

"How so?"

"Slattery's backers are demanding results and the Doctor isn't coming through to their satisfaction. He's ambitious, but, not tenacious; forever the academic and this is not sitting well with the Chinese. They're not interested in science for the sake of science. They're interested in the military application of Slattery's work. They want results and they want them now."

"And this is according to Piero"?

"Yes."

"Why did he reveal all of this to you and how did he find out about your, you know, your position with the government? He certainly wouldn't have come to you with all of this unless he knew who and what you were."

"Well, don't be put out by the fact that he came to me. He explained that it was imperative for him to take an opportunity that he was looking for, to stop the Foundation from continuing their research and development. He felt that you were too close to him and that it would have compromised your safety if he went to you. He knew something was up when he met you at the Foundation after your encounter on the road overlooking the compound. He kept his eye on you and made some deductions, all correct, about me."

"That's it?"

"That's what he told me, but I don't buy it."

"What do you think".

"I think he did an amazingly brilliant bit of hacking into highly classified government records to find out who I was. I don't know who this kid really is, but, I'm damned glad he's on our side."

"I agree. I've never bought into his orphan from China explanation. I've just never figured out if he believes it or if it's just some sort of cover for something else.'

"I think he's got a story to tell, but, I don't know if we'll ever hear it."

"Right now, I just wish he would get back here."

Jo walked over to the window which faced out to the front parking lot and road. She pulled the curtain aside as if expecting to see the now familiar yellow motorcycle. Downstairs was very active with customers beginning to make their way in as the dinner hour approached. Still, no Piero. It was growing dark and the parking lot was illuminated with a few lights scattered here and there. Jo continued her vigil.

"Don't worry, I'm sure he's OK," remarked Fiona.

"I'm concerned that he went back to the compound. It's the only place he could have gone. He must have gone there to do something or get something and that could be a problem. You don't have any idea about that, do you"?

"No. He contacted me, but, didn't go into detail. I guess that's what this rendezvous is about."

Just then, Jo heard the sound of a motorcycle coming into the front parking lot. As she looked out the window, she could see the yellow cycle pass under one of the lights on its way to the rear of the building.

"He's here!"

They heard the shed doors slam shut and Piero's footsteps as he ran up the staircase. He burst through the door in a hurried and agitated state which was totally out of character.

"Where have you been?" Jo demanded.

"I went to the compound."

"What in the hell is the matter with you? You know it's getting dangerous there."

"I'll explain later. Right now we have to go."

As he was speaking he continued to walk across the room to the closet, clutching a small metal case. He unlocked the door and grabbed a duffle bag from the back of the closet. Jo took note that it had already been packed, so, whatever was happening had been planned for and expected by Piero. It occurred to her that he may have been the one who precipitated the events in which they now all found themselves. He indicated that he was going down to the pub to have a word with the staff.

"We'll take the Jag." exclaimed Fiona.

"Jo, where is the pistol?"

"It's in my briefcase."

"Let me have it and the extra magazine."

Jo reached into her briefcase retrieving the two items and, handing them over to Fiona. She was relieved to get rid of them, but, considering the circumstances, her aversion to firearms was quickly disappearing.

Her friend quickly checked the spare magazine. She removed the one in the gun, checked it and replaced it. She then pulled back the action, released it, chambering a bullet and flipped on the safety. All of this was done with the speed and expertise of an individual well acquainted with the use of such a weapon. Fiona took notice of Jo's surprise and with the gun still in her hand stared at her with an expression as if to say, "Yes, this is what and who I am".

Piero returned from downstairs.

"Is there a problem?", asked Jo.

"No. I just wanted to give some instructions to the staff in case anyone comes asking about us."

"I think it's time to get the hell out of here", exclaimed Fiona.

Piero slung the strap of the duffle bag over his shoulder. As they proceeded toward the rear door of the apartment, Jo grabbed him by the arm.

"What's in the case?", she asked.

"The stuff that dreams are made of or the seeds of man's destruction. Perhaps both."

She was taken aback by his answer, but, there was no time to ponder it. As Fiona said, they had to get the hell out of there. An explanation would have to wait for a more suitable time.

They went quickly down to the shed and opened the door. Right now, time was not to be wasted. The top of the Jag was down so Piero hopped into the back and Jo took the front passenger seat. As they backed out, Jo took note of the other two vehicles left behind.

"What about the Mini and the motorcycle?

"Don't worry. No one will get to see them. I left instructions with the pub staff and they'll cover for us", Piero reassured her.

"They don't know what's going on, do they?", Jo asked.

"No, but they like and trust me and are suspicious of Slattery and hostile as to the goings on at the Foundation. Don't worry. They'll help us out."

"At least it'll give us some time", observed Fiona.

The Jag came around from the back of the pub, through the parking lot and accelerated down the road, disappearing into the darkness of the night. No one looked back to observe the black Rover entering the parking lot that they had just left.

Fiona made her way through the maze of dark, country roads. The night was black and moonless, but, the stars formed a twinkling canopy of almost unbroken bright white. Jo sat back, the cool wind blowing through her hair, forgetting the problems of the moment, absorbed in the majesty of it all. In her contemplation she reflected back on some of the things that she had experienced since coming to Cambridge and that, somehow, she knew that the work of the Foundation was focused on not only the known, but, the yet to be known. It was possible that Slattery had found a window, existing in the present, but, giving those who held the secret, a look into the future, revealing the secrets that man has yearned to know from the time the first earthly creature, capable of reason, looked at the night sky and wondered. But, this time it was not her mission to act as a detached scientist. She was here to stop whatever it was that the Foundation was involved in. The young man's warning as to the contents of the case echoed in her mind.

Piero leaned forward and tapped Fiona on the shoulder.

"Slow down and stay right where the road splits, about a mile up ahead."

Fiona came to the spot where the road divided and turned off onto what turned out to be a narrow, hilly and winding road.

"Go about five more miles", directed Piero.

The going was somewhat slow, but, after ten or fifteen minutes her passenger pointed to a spot off the shoulder of the road.

"Stop over there".

Fiona followed his instruction and pulled the Jag off the road. Except for the gravel crunching under the wheels of the car and the subdued hum of the engine, there was dead quiet. The headlights of the car cut through the darkness revealing a security gate.

"Now what?"

"Flash your lights, one long and two short."

Fiona complied and the gate slid open.

CHAPTER TWENTY-THREE

"Pull over to the left and park in the space on the other side of the bushes."

After the car was parked the trio got out and Fiona and Jo waited for Piero to lead the way.

"Over here and be careful", he called out as he led them up a foot path to their ultimate destination which was not yet in sight. Great care had to be taken as the path was not lit and the lack of moonlight created such a darkness that, when one looked down, they could not even see their own feet.

"Here, let me put this on before we break our necks", declared Fiona as she pulled a small flashlight from her purse and aimed the thin beam of light ahead of them and up the hill.

"Much better."

They continued the climb up the steep path, as Jo calculated the distance to be some thirty or forty yards, until a house came into view. The outline of the structure could be seen in silhouette against the night sky. At that moment, a light went on above the entrance door illuminating enough of the front of the building so that she could identify it as a two story stone structure common in the Cotswold area of England. Piero walked to the far corner of the front of the property and stood at the edge of an embankment which provided a view of the road leading to the house. He stood there for a moment and scanned the route that they had just traveled as if expecting to see something, perhaps the headlights of the black Rover. But, there was nothing; at least for now.

After satisfying himself that there was nothing to see, he turned his attention back to the house and to the man who had appeared in the doorway. He was Asian, Chinese Jo surmised as that would be consistent with Piero's background and those affiliated with the Foundation. Small and diminutive would be an accurate description. He couldn't have been more than five feet, four inches tall. The top of his head was totally bald and there was the typical fringe of hair, silver-grey, which had grown to shoulder length. He wore a light brown pajama-like outfit with a Mandarin collar. As she drew closer, she could see that his face was clean shaven, old and weathered, but, his eyes, unbespectacled, were clear and intense. Yet unlike Slattery's, they revealed an inner serenity.

"I am Chan. Welcome to my home."

His greeting was spoken in a decidedly British accent.

As they entered the house, Jo continued to scrutinize their host. By his general appearance, she estimated that he was in his 80's, but his voice was strong and clear as a bell, giving no hint of such age. As he escorted them to the sitting room of the house, she noticed that he moved with the quickness, grace and agility of a young man.

He turned to Piero.

"You've brought the item?"

"Yes. It's in the case."

"Good, give it to me."

The old man took the case and went down a hall and through a doorway which Jo believed led to a cellar.

"Would you care to fill us in?", Fiona inquired of Piero in a rather impatient tone of voice.

"Please, I appreciate your curiosity, but, all in due time", was his response.

This reply did not please her friend and she expressed her lack of satisfaction.

"Let me make myself very clear. We have reached a level in this matter where our lives are on the line and these enigmatic non-explanations of yours simply will not do. Sometimes I don't think you understand the nature of the people we're dealing with."

"Believe me Fiona, I understand full well who we are dealing with, more than you know."

Before the verbal jousting could continue, the old man returned from his task and turned his attention to Piero.

"Did you take care of things at the Foundation?"

"We have to go back."

"What about Slattery?"

"At this moment, I don't know."

"That will all have to be dealt with."

"Miss Clark and Doctor Russo, I hope that you will forgive my momentary lapse as host, but, as you can understand these questions needed to be answered. After all, we are seeking a common goal."

Chan looked toward Fiona.

Do you think that you were followed?"

"I don't believe so."

Piero interrupted.

"No. I am sure. Nobody will come for us until it is cleared with their government. But, that could happen quickly, especially as things now stand."

"It is probably happening as we speak. In fact, I would not doubt that we shall have an encounter tonight", observed Chan.

"Then we should prepare", exclaimed Fiona, with a sense of urgency.

"No. The three of you shall retire upstairs", responded Chan.

"And then?", Fiona asked.

"And then we put the lights out and wait."

"I don't think that's a good idea."

"We would do well to trust Chan's judgment", Piero suggested.

Piero's comments again brought Fiona's displeasure to the fore.

"I appreciate your insight into our situation, but, I don't think a good night's sleep is what any of us need right now."

Fiona displayed the gun which Jo had turned over to her earlier.

"Maybe it would be best if I stood watch with this."

"That would not be acceptable", asserted Chan in a calm yet authoritative tone.

"There will be no guns used by anyone who is a guest in this house. Now, the hour is late and I must ask all of you to retire to your designated rooms. Piero will escort you upstairs and take you to your quarters."

As they ascended the stairs, Chan called to Fiona.

"Miss Clark, I have allowed you to keep your weapon. Please make sure that you do not use it."

Fiona looked back at the old man standing at the foot of the stairs, but, did not respond.

When they reached the top of the stairs, Fiona grabbed Piero by the arm.

"I don't like this. I don't like this, at all."

Piero turned to her.

"Don't worry. I know Chan. We are guests in his house and he will not let any harm come to us."

"I hope you're right."

"I am."

Jo observed the exchange between the two, but, said nothing.

Piero directed the two women to their rooms.

"Good night and please keep your lights off", he instructed.

"Where's Chan?", Jo asked.

"Preparing", was Piero's response.

Jo didn't understand his response nor its implications, but, asked nothing further and retired to her bedroom to await the events of the night.

CHAPTER TWENTY-FOUR

The two lay there staring up into the darkness of the room. The night continued in its eerie quite. Fiona was the first to break the silence.

"I wonder what in bloody hell our friend Chan is up to."

"I don't know, but, I wish I had the same confidence in him that Piero does."

"Just when I thought I had somewhat of a grip on this whole thing, a new player enters the picture. He is an odd fellow and I just don't know what to make of him", observed Fiona.

Jo did not respond and drifted in and out of an uneasy sleep. The day had been an exhausting one more from the psychological pressure rather than the physical activity. She didn't know how much time had passed when she heard Fiona's voice which seemed like a distant whisper.

"Jo, wake up."

"What, what is it?"

"I don't know. I was half asleep myself."

They both arose from bed as quietly and cautiously as they could.

"Leave the lights off", Fiona instructed her friend.

They made their way over to the open window which faced the back of the house and looked out trying to avoid being seem by anyone who might be lurking about. If Fiona had heard anything, the likeliest source would have been the back garden which their bedroom window overlooked.. They both strained to see through the darkness. There was nothing, at least nothing that was apparent. Fiona gave up the search and walked back to her bed, picking up the gun and flashlight which she had left on the nightstand.

"Enough of this. I'm going downstairs and have a look."

"Do you think it's wise to disregard Chan?"

"Chan seems to be a good sort, but, to rely on anybody but yourself, in this business, is a good way to get killed. You might want to remember that in the future."

Jo thought Fiona's admonishment to be curious. It was as if she were suggesting that the present adventure was more than that. That it was a test, a recruitment to bring her into the fold that her old friend and Peter had been a part of for the last ten years. But, there wasn't time for such thoughts. Not now.

"Follow me", ordered Fiona, as she opened the bedroom door just enough to get a view of the hallway. There seemed to be no activity. Piero's door was shut, but there was no way of telling if he was still in his room or had joined Chan downstairs.

They left heir bedroom and proceeded down the hall to the staircase. The light cast by the small lamp on the hallway table ended at the head of the stairs. Fiona switched on her small flashlight, keeping it directed down toward the steps to both light their way and to prevent, as much as possible, disclosing their presence.

After slowly descending the staircase, they reached the bottom and momentarily stood motionless in the living room while Fiona scanned the area with her flashlight. Luck was with them as a couple of decorative candles were revealed, on a table, next to which lay a few wooden matches. The candles would prove useful. Jo walked over and lit one of them. It wasn't as good as the flashlight, but, did provide some necessary illumination.

"What now?", she asked Fiona. Her friend did not respond but, rather, walked over to the front door and tested it; turning the knob and running the flashlight beam around the edge.

"The door seems secure and there aren't any signs of forced entry", she concluded.

She then walked across the living room, past the dining area and into the kitchen to the door leading to the rear garden. Once again, there was nothing suspicious about the door, although she took notice that, unlike the front entry light which was on, the light over the back entrance had been switched off. Fiona immediately flipped off the flashlight as well as the safety on her gun. It would be difficult to see, but, the flashlight would make her an easy target for anyone lurking out in the bushes. She would have to deal with the darkness, but, so would any predator laying in wait for her. She crouched down, pressing herself against the wall next to the door and gripped the flashlight between her teeth, freeing one hand. She reached over and turned the latch ever so slowly. There was a click. The stillness of the night amplified the sound. She held her breath and listened. She didn't detect any noise or motion coming from the garden. Her hand moved up to the door knob. She turned it and pushed the back door open just enough to get a view of the garden. All appeared quiet. She stood up keeping as low a profile as possible and proceeded outside, gun in one hand, flashlight, still off, in the other. Her eyes had adjusted to the darkness, more so than when they had first arrived. The night was crystal clear and she could make out shapes, when she got close enough, and silhouettes of objects seen against the bright canopy of stars. She moved ahead cautiously. She was distracted by the underbrush scratching against her leg when, suddenly, she stumbled over something in the thicket. She struggled to maintain her balance. As she did so, she stepped on the unseen thing that she had just tripped over. A body! It was a body. The thought raced through her head. She focused the flashlight beam on the body and moved the beam op to the face which seemed to be in a state of peaceful sleep. Further examination, however, revealed an ugly purplish bruise on the right temple apparently from a single blow deftly, accurately and skillfully applied resulting in unconsciousness, hemorrhaging and death.

Fiona recognized the unfortunate individual as one of the Asians that they had seen in the black Rover. That accounted for one. But, the second was of immediate concern. She doused the flashlight and moved away from the body to avoid being located from the noise that she had made from stumbling around. *But, how?* Chan. It must have been Chan who killed the man laying at her feet.

Jo did not hear the brief but intense activity that was taking place in the back garden. She was growing anxious and impatient. There did not seem to be any imminent danger and this looked to be an opportunity, presenting itself, for her to explore the cellar where Chan had taken the case and its contents.

The candle didn't provide much light, but, it did allow her to find her way to the door and staircase. She tested the door and although she had not considered that it might be locked, she was surprised to find that it was not. *Was this an oversight?* Hardly, she surmised. Likely, it was an accommodation by Chan to allow them to discover some of the secrets contained in the house, but, only those things which he wished them to know. She opened the door and took a single and cautious step inside. She stopped and moved the candle up and down and back and for the in front of her to determine how to navigate her way down the stairs. The staircase was long and steep. It was open on the right hand side with no banister, just a long drop which would, likely, be a fatal fall should one lose their footing and find themselves plunging into the darkness to the floor below. The stairs, however, were built flush to the wall on the left hand side which would provide safety during a descent. She held the candle out in front of her, as far as possible, desperately trying to maximize her ability to see where the next step would take her. The stairs were steep, shallow and treacherous, but, she proceeded to make her way, groping along the wall with her free hand making sure not to lean against it should it unexpectedly end with disastrous consequences.

Fiona, finding the body of one of the Asians, but, not the other, became concerned for the welfare of Jo who she thought had remained in the living room waiting for her to return. She hurried back into the house and with the beam of the flashlight, scanned the area where she had left her friend. Jo was nowhere to be seen. Fiona refrained from calling out. Just having the flashlight on was taking a chance. Going down the hall leading from the living room, she found the cellar door open. Proceeding to the entrance, she peered, cautiously into the darkness, her small flashlight illuminating just enough for her to see the precipitous staircase. Jo had made her way to the far end of the downstairs room and was preparing to do some investigation when she suddenly heard footsteps coming from the top of the stairs. She immediately doused the candle, hoping that she had not been seen. There was a support column directly to the left of her and she groped her way toward it. It offered her a refuge of sorts, but, only until the intruder had made their way to her. She knew, then, she would have no choice but to act. Alternatives began to present themselves. *Could it be Fiona?* There was no way of telling unless she called out. That would be foolish and, possibly, fatal. She had no weapon and dare not move, in the darkness, to search for one. No, there was nothing to do but to remain where she was, struggling not to make any sound whatsoever and to make her body as narrow as possible so that the column gave her maximum cover. She was anxious and her lungs screamed for her to take in more air, but, she had to suffer the discipline of short, shallow and quiet breaths, lest she disclose her presence. Whoever it had made their way downstairs and was proceeding across the room, cautiously and in her direction. She did not see the source of the light, but, judged the location of the person by where the light was aiming. She thought to herself how useful that fireplace poker would be right at this moment. As she sorted through her options she came to the conclusion that she was at least big and strong enough, together with the element of surprise to knock her adversary off their feet and make good her escape out of the basement. Time was up. She made her move and lunged at the virtually unseen figure just as it passed her hiding place. At the instant of making contact, she discerned that whoever it was, was of relatively short stature. She had hardly enough time for the word "Fiona" to cross her thoughts when she felt a sharp blow to her solar plexus. The wind was instantly knocked out of her and she fell to the ground in the proverbial heap. She lay there desperately trying to catch her breath. From behind the light, shining in her face, she heard the welcome voice of her friend.

"Jo, just stay down for a bit. You'll be all right."

Finally, with the assistance of Fiona, she was able to get back on her feet.

There was no further time to waste. They wanted to do some exploration of the room before they were discovered. Fiona cast the beam of the flashlight along the upper edge of the walls, just below the ceiling.

"There don't seem to be any windows to the outside, so let's find a light and have a look around."

As Fiona scanned the premises, still clutching her gun, it appeared that there were a series of work tables and suspended over each was a large light fixture. She walked up to the closest table, reached up and turned on the light. It flickered for a moment as the florescent tubes slowly illuminated. The light disclosed a few rough sketches spread out on the work area. They appeared to be a series of technical or mechanical drawings.

"I recognize that one", commented Jo, pointing to the far end of the table.

"It's similar to an illustration in the book of a Da Vinci sketch. I believe it's a drawing of an artillery shell with fins, or something like that."

She picked up the drawing and held it nearer to the light for a closer inspection.

"This drawing is not laid out in the same way as the one in the book. The subject matter is the same, but, it's laid out in a different configuration and the artwork seems to be finer, less crude; different, but, the same. This isn't a copy or a replica of the one in the book. This is an original."

Fiona took the sketch from Jo. She felt the paper and ran her fingers over the surface. She then held it up to the light, examining both the back and front of the curious item.

"You're right. This is original and contemporary. Why would someone engage in such an activity? Perhaps, for some reason, practicing."

"Perhaps recalling", suggested Jo.

Fiona looked at her friend quizzically, but, said nothing in response.

While Fiona had been examining the one drawing, Jo had continued to scan some of the other documents on the same work table.

"This is interesting."

"What is?", queried Fiona.

"If you line up what's here on the table, in order of apparent complexity or design, you arrive at an illustrated evolution of the artillery shell, from the time of da Vinci's original drawing, to the present."

"You're right. Nothing that high tech, but, certainly the most recent appear to be circa World War II. I would think that there might be more around here if we look hard enough. What's more astonishing is that this is da Vinci's work taken and expanded upon."

The two women were deeply engrossed in their examination of the drawings that they had discovered and were startled by the voice coming out of the darkness on the other side of the room not illuminated by the single overhead light.

"I see that you ladies have taken it upon yourselves to explore my humble quarters. Well, do not apologize. You would have disappointed me had you not done so. Those drawings, that you have been examining, seem to be of considerable interest to you."

Chan stepped into the light and revealed himself. Jo took the opportunity to respond to Chan.

"It is true that they are interesting, in fact they're incongruity is more than interesting, it's fascinating. The one seems to be based on da Vinci's drawing. There are consistencies, yet, in some important ways the drawings are different. It's not a copy or an exact reproduction and the others couldn't be copies because they don't exist in the historical record."

"That is because they are not copies. They are drawn from memory", responded Chan.

"From whose memory?"

"From the memory of the one who originally created them."

"I don't understand."

"All in good time, Doctor. And Ms. Clark, you can put your firearm away. There is no longer any need for it."

"What about the other Asian? There were two from the Foundation and I only discovered one of them out back."

"Let us just say that neither presents a problem, any longer."

Fiona reluctantly placed the gun in her jacket pocket, keeping it at the ready.

During the exchange between Fiona and Chan, Jo was walking about the room. She observed other tables or work areas, some with drawings, recognizable and unrecognizable. There were paintings, both classical and modern or abstract and architectural models that encompassed designs of the past, the present and those that were seemingly advanced beyond anything that existed today. It was a place that contained works and representations that spanned the ages of past, present and seemingly, future.

"I see that our little workshop has captured your interest, Dr. Russo", commented Chan.

"My interest and my curiosity. Is there more?"

"There is"

"Would you show us?"

"Much has been destroyed. Most of what remains, you see before you in the confines of this room."

"But why destroy these things?"

"If you reflect on your question, you will conclude that the danger is too great to allow such evidence to remain as a clue to those who would misuse it. Even though such knowledge may lie dormant in the human mind, there is that part of the nature of the species which makes it ill-equipped to be trusted with that knowledge. The intellectual capacity of human kind, as expressed in and through the things which man creates, must be allowed to evolve as the human species and its civilization evolves in order to use such material and scientific advances wisely. Even in present times, which we like to think of as the modern world, we see, all around is, technical knowledge being subjugated to our primitive instincts. What you see before you is only an infinitesimal part of the larger universe of possibilities and of those things which could be created. Weapons, of course being the focus of the Foundation and world domination being the motivation."

"Then you're suggesting, or, should I say asserting, that genetic memory is more than just a theory and that Slattery and the Foundation had established that the phenomenon was based on empirical science."

"I will let you draw your own conclusions from what you see before you."

"That would be more of a leap of faith", Fiona commented.

"These drawings and the models raise some interesting prospects, but, are hardly conclusive."

"Your skepticism is well taken, Ms. Clark. Perhaps, a demonstration will convince you as to the authenticity of what you see before you and its ultimate meaning."

"Your gun, please", requested Chan, with an outstretched hand.

Fiona looked at him and hesitated to carry out his request.

"I can assure you that your firearm is no longer necessary while you remain in this house."

Fiona withdrew the pistol from her pocket, made sure that it was unloaded and reluctantly handed it over to Chan.

"Thank you. Now, both of you come with me to that table at the far end of the room."

They walked over to the table indicated by Chang and watched as he pulled back a tarp which had covered it. Built into the table, at its center, was an innocuous looking, smooth, dull gray plate, which appeared to be of metal and looked to be about two feet in diameter. Underneath the table, on the floor, was a second device of some sort. It was square in shape, perhaps two feet by two feet and only six, or so, inches high. The combination of the two devices, together, reminded Jo, oddly, of the square and circle associated with Vitruvian Man. The Box or device under the table was not visibly connected to the plate and there did not seem to be a power source, with cables, leading to either one of them. She was sure that this was probably some sort of electromagnetic device, yet, its appearance and configuration were unlike anything that she had seen before. Chang took the gun and put it on the plate. He then passed his hand over what must have been some sort of sensor situated between the plate and the edge of the table. This was, apparently to activate the mechanism, but, there was no sound, only a faint glow emitting from the metallic plate. He then passed his hand over the sensor for a second time causing the plate to glow with a slightly greater intensity. Still there was no sound and although the plate was illuminated, there was no discernible heat being given off. The gun began to rise off the plate and stabilized when it had reached a height of six, or so, feet above the table. It remained there until Chan reversed the process at which time the gun slowly descended to its original resting place atop the plate.

"An electro-magnetic force field", stated Jo.

"Ah, much more than that", Chan responded.

"How can we be sure of that?", interrupted Fiona.

"Perhaps this will be a more convincing demonstration even for one as cynical as yourself Ms. Clark."

Chan walked over to an area that held some cages containing a few lab animals. He brought one over and place it on the table. In a cage labeled "Einstein" was a white guinea pig.

"Einstein, how cute", remarked Fiona, sarcastically.

"This little fellow is more than whimsy. He is most unique and aptly named as you will see. He is in fact the first living organism that has truly defied gravity with-out the use of means such as freefall, super conductors, electro-magnetic devices or processes which effect the water molecules of organisms, such as has been done with frogs."

Chan than took a large clear glass cylinder, open at both ends and about four feet in height. He removed "Einstein" from his cage and placed him on the plate, holding him there.

"Doctor Russo, would you assist and kindly place the cylinder over the plate."

Jo complied and as she did so, Chan released his grip on the small creature and withdrew his hand, leaving the guinea pig on the plate confined by the cylinder.

Chan repeated the procedure as he had done with Fiona's pistol, only this time the demonstration was infinitely more dramatic. As Chan increased the power, the little animal gradually rose off the plate to an area halfway up the height of the cylinder, where he remained suspended in thin air, his movements causing him to slowly tumble. Jo and Fiona stared in silent astonishment. At this point, both of the women realized that they were observing something that they had never seen before, perhaps, something that, save for Chan and Piero, no one had ever seen before.

"I trust that this has alleviated some of your skepticism", remarked Chan, directing his comments to Fiona.

"But, how is this done?"asked Jo.

"It is much too complicated to explain and even if I chose to do so, the greatest minds in physics today would only be able to comprehend what has been done, relative to the present knowledge of science and not how it is done. Simply stated, gravity, or, the force that we commonly label as gravity, has ceased to exist within the area affected by the field contained within the cylinder."

"And you can control it; its power and the extent of its effects?"

"Yes."

"If you've been able to do this and neutralize gravity in a select and controlled way, then what about time space and even quantum teleportation?"

"Before I answer your question, let me take care of this little fellow."

Chan turned his attention back to "Einstein" who was still floating midway in the cylinder. With a couple of waves of his hand over the sensor, gravity was reintroduced and the guinea pig descended to the surface of the plate, removed and safely tucked back into his cage.

"Now, Doctor Russo, as to your question. What I have shown you is all that you will see. Everything else that has resulted from the knowledge and labors exercised in these humble quarters has been or will, shortly, be destroyed. Other than that, you are free to draw your own conclusions."

"But, you can't do that. All of what you have developed and created here will be lost."

"To the contrary. It has simply not as yet been found. At least, not in the way intended."

"You say intended. Intended by who or what?"

"Ah! I'm afraid that goes much beyond our immediate course of inquiry."

"And what of Piero? Where does he fit into all of this? Is he the source? Where is he?"

"You have many questions. I will answer your last. He has gone."

"And the metal case?"

"He has taken it with him."

"Is he the source of all of this?"

"In a manner of speaking."

"I don't understand."

"I wouldn't expect you to. You see, Dr. Russo, in the natural order of things, each of us live in the present and is merely a conduit or a link between the past and the future. The young man that you know as Piero is more than that. He is not just a link, but, his knowledge and intellectual capacity is a unity of all three elements of time and increase as he matures. How far it will reach is impossible to predict, but, as he grows older, these powers accelerate in their development."

"Then, he's responsible for what we've seen?"

Yes and much more. But, these are only toys which are replications of the known past or inventions which exceed present day science only by a few centuries. Unfortunately, such material objects comprise the sum total of that which attracted Dr. Slattery and my countrymen who sponsored the Foundation. The ultimate value of Piero's potential knowledge is the possibility that he could answer questions as to the origins of man or knowledge as to pre history or things even further in the past. As to the future, he has shown development there as you saw from the demonstration with Einstein. If future memory were to abruptly stop, it could mean, simply, that his genetic memory has limitations. It could also mean that at that point, the human species has become extinct either by chance or by design. It is our belief that the memory or remembrance is there. It is a matter of recall."

"But, if Piero possesses such abilities how could the Foundation allow him his freedom or, for that matter, let him out of China?"

"Yes, how?", asserted Fiona.

"It is the essence of simplicity. They simply did not know. Piero was born in China during the earlier stages of the experimentation. There were others before him, but, the results were unsuccessful and they were disposed of."

"Killed?" inquired Jo.

"Yes."

"Piero was left from one of the groups and I was his guardian and mentor assigned to observe his development. As he progressed in age, it was apparent that he was special; that quite possibly he was to develop into what my government had been looking for after years of trial and failure."

"But, why him and none of the others that came before him?"

"That is a question that still cannot be answered except to speculate that there is some as yet undetectable anomaly in the DNA. It was just before the arrival of Dr. Slattery in China that the situation turned grave."

"How so?"

"I could not allow the government to learn of Piero's advancement and that he might very well be the success that they, for many tears, had been looking for. To do so would render him to the status of a laboratory animal and to allow those in power to extract his knowledge for their own nefarious ends. But, to hide his abilities would put him in the category of just being another experimental failure and render him useless to suffer the same fate as his predecessors. As good fortune would have it, Dr. Slattery interceded before a decision had to be made with regard to the course of action to be taken for the boy's protection. The Doctor felt some affinity for him and suggested that he bring Piero back to Cambridge to be raised in England. I don't know the motivation. Perhaps he felt that the boy might be the son that he never had and would provide him with some sort of personal legacy. Whatever the reason, it solved what was looking to be an insurmountable problem. By that time, Piero, himself, knew that he was unique and that he had to keep that fact a secret. He and Dr. Slattery left for England and I followed shortly thereafter."

"So, for these years, you've assisted him in carrying on this charade."

"Yes. It is only within the confines of these walls that the truth is revealed."

"And what of the Foundation at this moment?", asked Fiona.

"During Piero's absence while you were waiting for him to return to the pub and before you came here, he was able to go back to the compound and to release the two pregnant women turning them over to our agents who, in turn, spirited them to an undisclosed location. But, there is more to be done which must be accomplished by the two of you and you must not fail. When you are finished with your mission, nothing must be left, nothing!"

Fiona fully understood the implication of Chang's statement. There could be nothing tangible left at the Foundation which could disclose or relate the nature of the work, including anyone who remained at the compound.

"And what of the evidence in China?" asked Jo.

"That will be disposed of by anti-government forces in the country."

"And you?"

"I will join my young friend and Einstein and the few creatures that you see here will be released to resume their place in nature. But, now you both must go. Here, you will need this."

Chan handed Fiona a glove fashioned of a thin rubbery material.

This will allow admittance to all of the areas at the compound. It's a facsimile of an authorized finger and hand print which we created in our modest workshop. I regret that you both did not have the opportunity to say your goodbyes to Piero, but, this is the way it must be. Come this way. There is an exit from this room directly to the outside."

As Chan turned to lead the women out, Jo grabbed him by the arm.

"You know so much, perhaps you know something of the death of Peter Simpson."

Chan paused for a moment, looking her directly in the eye.

"That is a subject that I had hoped we would not breach. But, to answer your question, yes, I do know."

"I want to know. Who killed him?"

There was a pause as the two stared silently at each other.

"It was Jack, wasn't it?

"Yes."

Chan's answer was a confirmation of what she had always suspected, but, hearing it caused a silent rage to well up within her.

Chan sensed her emotions and cautioned her.

CHAPTER TWENTY-FOUR

"You must set your passions aside for the task ahead. You cannot fail."

Jo heard Chan's admonition, but, they were just words, just sound without meaning and couldn't intrude her consciousness which was filled with thoughts of Peter and revenge against those who took him away.

"We have to go, now", she exclaimed in a forceful tone.

Chan understood the source of her urgency.

"Remember", he said, "you must complete your mission. Nothing can interfere."

Jo briefly glanced back at Chan with a preoccupied look and stepped out into the darkness of the night.

As Fiona was about to follow, Chan spoke his final words to her.

"You understand what you must do. I'm afraid that, on this night, you will not only be pitted against those that guard the secrets of the Foundation, but, also against your friend's state of mind."

"Don't worry Chan. I know my friend. She'll come through."

"I believe that you are right", Chan responded with a slight but knowing smile.

Fiona joined Jo and both walked quickly to the car. Fiona walked to the rear of the Jag.

"Wait a second while I get something out of the boot. She pulled a large valise out and closed the lid, dropping the bag in front of Jo.

"What's this?"

"A few little items which might come in handy."

Fiona reached in and pulled out a .38 caliber snub nose revolver, handing it to Jo.

"Take this. It's uncomplicated and has five shots. We don't know what we'll be facing. So, if you have to use it, don't hesitate and make your shots count. By the way, it has a maximum accuracy of up to fifty feet, so, don't get into any long distance shootouts."

"I'll try to remember that."

Jo took the gun and stuffed it into her jacket pocket.

"What else did you bring along."

Fiona grabbed the bag and threw it into the back seat.

"We'll go over that on the way. Right now we've got to get out of here."

They both hastily got into the car. Fiona started the engine, hit the gas and accelerated rapidly down the road. They were no more than a mile along their journey when they heard a powerful explosion behind them. They turned around to see the site where Chan's house had stood enveloped in flame and smoke, a dramatic and fiery beacon standing alone in the blackness of the night.

"Well, Chan's taken care of one site where no evidence will be found. It'll probably go down as an accidental explosion from leaking gas," remarked Fiona.

"It didn't seem like he had the time to clear the house", observed Jo.

"Oh, I'm sure Chan and Einstein are just fine. You can rest assured that he didn't show us all of the toys he had lurking about."

Fiona turned her full attention to the road. The trip to the compound had to be made as fast as possible. There was much to be done and time was not on their side. Dawn would soon be breaking.

CHAPTER TWENTY-FIVE

The Jag cut its way through the darkness of the English countryside, the two occupants resolute in accomplishing the task before them. Fiona broke the silence and shouted instructions to Jo over the noise of the engine and rushing wind.

"Jo, reach back and bring that bag up here."

She twisted around and groped for the handles, in the darkness, swinging the large and heavy object over the seatback and placing it on her lap.

"What else have you got in here?"

"There's a small flashlight, pull it out and take a look."

Jo complied with her friend's instruction taking out the flashlight and inspecting the rest of the contents. She recoiled and exclaimed:

"What in the hell! Are these bombs?"

"Very good. Actually their plastic explosives attached to timing devices."

"Are they safe?"

"Yeah. Just don't flip any of the switches", responded Fiona with an impish grin.

"Zip it up and I'll go over how to use them when we get to where we're going. Don't worry, it's simple."

"Have you figured out how we're going to get in?", Jo inquired of her friend.

"Not through the front door, I assure you. We're going up that road where you met Piero at the back border of the compound."

"What about the security system."

"Piero rigged it during his brief visit to the Foundation just before he met us at the pub. It appears to be functioning, but, isn't. I don't know how he did in such a short time, but, I've no doubt that he did. Amazing fellow."

"Yes, he is", reflected Jo.

It wasn't long before they found themselves on the familiar stretch of road that Jo had used to observe the compound, early on. So relatively little time had passed since that day, yet, so much had happened to change her world. Only this time it wouldn't be Piero who they would be encountering but, rather, the unknown dangers that awaited them on the grounds and in the buildings of the Serpentine Foundation.

It was early morning, 3:12 A. M., to be precise, when they arrived at their destination, the hillside road traveled by Jo when she observed the compound at the point where she first encountered Piero. Fiona doused the lights as the Jag slowed down and pulled off onto the shoulder. She reached for the bag and started to pull things out.

"Here, put these on", she instructed Jo, handing her a pair of black coveralls, a black watch cap and a pair of black running shoes.

"We don't have everything I'd like, but, we should be able to make due. Let me show you how to operate these bombs. They're safe to handle until they've been activated. It's pretty simple. You set the digital timer with this button. Depress it until the desired number of seconds or minutes is displayed. It goes up to one hour, but, that's way beyond what we'll need. When you've set the timer, you flip the to set the time running and then get the hell away from wherever your at as fast as possible. Take this backpack. There are five devices in it."

Fiona then pulled out a second backpack.

"There are five more in here. Each of the packs has the minimum number to do what we have to do. One each for the wood frame lab and the brick building where you saw the two Asian women. Piero told me that it was a combination dormitory and clinic but doesn't contain any extraordinary or elaborate equipment. That leaves one for the house and two for the bunker. All of the buildings will be destroyed, except for the bunker, but, it'll be sufficiently gutted so there won't be evidence left as to what went on there. We'll stick together, if possible and double up on the explosives, but, if we separate we'll each have enough to do the job. Check for the revolver."

"Right here", Jo responded, displaying the gun.

"Good, keep it in your hand and if you you're doing something tuck it away someplace on you. Don't ever lay it down out of reach and never hesitate to use it, no matter who you have to shoot and that includes Slattery. Let's get on with it!"

They descended the embankment and began rapidly traversing the two hundred, or so, yards of pasture which lay behind the rear fence of the compound. There was none of the familiar noise that Jo was accustomed to. No planes, no cars, no people, just silence. She was conscious of the sound of her own breathing which became slightly labored as they got closer to the compound. She also felt anxious in being exposed as she crossed the large expanse of land, even with the assurances that Piero had neutralized the security system. What would happen, she thought, if someone decided to scan the property with a night vision scope, improbable, but, not impossible. No. She had to get those thoughts out of her mind and press on.

"So far, so good. Looks like Piero did his job", whispered Fiona.

"I know this place has motion sensors, so, if they hadn't been neutralized we'd probably be dead by now. That's one obstacle out of the way."

Fiona took a pair of wire cutters, from her knapsack and tossed them at the fence. They struck the metallic barrier with no apparent result.

"Good. The current's been interrupted. Keep a sharp eye while I cut through this thing."

Jo scanned the area looking for any movement and listening for any sound which might signal danger, gun at the ready, not knowing what to expect or how she would react. She turned her attention to the main house and saw no lights on. She couldn't, however, see the other side of the house containing Slattery's office and library and it was more than likely that some activity was going on in there. It was reasonable to assume that Slattery and Jack knew that something was amiss when their hit men did not return to report that they had carried out their mission.

Fiona had completed cutting the hole in the fence.

"Let's get moving."

There was an understandable urgency in her voice.

"We'll stay together, for now and do the bunker first."

They proceeded, quietly and rapidly, to the building which always gave the compound a decidedly ominous look. The darkness was, at best, unnerving considering that it was a certainty that Jack was somewhere, lurking about. The positive factor was that the area was not lit up like a Christmas Tree by motion detector lights. Slattery and company had determined that it was best to remain inconspicuous and that meant no lights; a decision that would contribute to their undoing.

When they reached the security door, Fiona pulled out the glove with the facsimile prints, experiencing a combination of both anxiety and anticipation. They heard the metallic sound of the lock disengaging.

"Well done, Piero", Fiona muttered to herself.

Jo's confidence grew with each successful step that they took. It did seem that, indeed, Piero had performed flawlessly, but, their mission was only beginning. They still had a long way to go and anything could happen to thwart their plans or, in the extreme, get them killed.

"Follow me in", Fiona ordered.

"We'll double the charges on this one."

Both entered the bunker cautiously, weapons at the ready, uncertain what to expect. Jo closed the door behind them so as not to betray their presence. She grabbed Fiona by the shoulder as they approached the elevator shaft.

"That damned elevator's going to be an announcement that we're her. Even with the thickness of these walls, you can here that electric motor all over the place. The sound must carry through the ventilation system. I've never looked, but, there's got to be a stairway somewhere in here."

A look behind the structure that housed the elevator disclosed another security door which opened onto a narrow staircase. The two descended to a second doorway which led into the room, now familiar to Jo and which housed the secrets of the Foundation. Fiona entered the almost too brightly lit room, pausing momentarily in order to familiarize herself in these new surroundings.

"What in bloody hell is this place?"

"My sentiments exactly, when Slattery took me down here. But, it gets better."

Jo went over to the chamber and executed the sequences to unlock it. Both stood back as the lid opened and the racks containing the small glass vials rose from the icy mist.

"Take a look". offered Jo, to her friend. What you're seeing is the answer to humanities greatest questions or the beginning of new and more dangerous ones. That's why none of this can be allowed to exist and why the remaining traces of it must be destroyed. I'm surprised that our governments didn't try to get their hands on some of the material."

"They did, but, Piero threatened to withhold his cooperation and that we could not afford. But, enough talk, we've got to get down to business. We'll stay together, for now and put four charges in this building.. Take two out of your bag and hang on to them. Well set those upstairs on the ground level."

Jo and Fiona proceeded to remove their back packs and each took out two of the explosive devices.

"Check your watch and synchronize it with mine", instructed Fiona.

"It's 3:21. All of the bombs should be set to go off at 4:00 A.M., sharp, so set each timer accordingly. That should give us enough time to do what we have to do with a little left over to get the hell out of here before everything goes up."

Just minutes ago, as the two were making their way across the back pasture, many things had run across Jo's mind. She thought of the unique events that had led her to be at this particular place, at this particular time. She had reviewed all of the possibilities as to what could go wrong and what would be the state of events when the sun rose on that day. It was certain that she would no longer be the person that she had been before coming to Cambridge two or three weeks ago. In fact, the metamorphosis was well under way. The fear and anxiety that she had anticipated was not there. Instead, there was a rush. She was no longer the scientist, thinking in the abstract, methodically and endlessly weighing the alternatives, many times bogged down into inaction because of the demands of others. No. There was none of this here, in the world she now found herself. This was different. She was released, perhaps elevated, to a more primitive state where the mind clears of all things except for the moment at hand. Where reflexes and motor skills reach a heightened level, where senses become more acute and where instinct replaces intellectual thought. One becomes like the jungle animal where all that matters is survival and the hunt and for that brief interval all other things of the world cease to exist.

Fiona took her two devices, putting one in the chamber and one at the back of the console housing the computer and set both of the timers.

"Jo, close the chamber, just in case anyone comes in here. The timing device wouldn't be effected by the temperature as Piero had disabled the system. Let's get upstairs and set the other two."

The two continued their task and two more of the devices were left to do their destruction. Only this time the number of minutes designated on the timers was reduced being a sobering reminder that time was against them.

The two women hurriedly exited the bunker, each of them pausing to briefly scan their surroundings for any signs of activity. There was none observed, but, this didn't serve to comfort them as it was odd that things appeared so quiet, even at this time of the morning, in light of the events at Chan's house. Certainly, by this time, both Slattery and Jack should have concluded that all had not gone as planned and the two should now be engaged in some alternative action. There was no doubt that they now had to increase their vigilance.

"They've got to be up to something", whispered Fiona.

As they changed their location relative to the main house, they noticed a single light illuminating one room of the house, the only indication that someone, other than themselves was in the compound. The light appeared to be coming from the library which housed the computer noticed by Fiona during their first meeting with Slattery.

"We've got to hurry", Fiona exclaimed and redistributed the devices, leaving Jo with two and herself with the remaining four.

"Take these two and set them in the other lab building. It looks deserted and you shouldn't run into any problems. Check your watch so that detonation is as close to 4:00 a.m. as you can get, but, you can't afford to be off by more than a few seconds. I'll take care of the residence building and the house. We've got to be out of here by 3:55."

As Jo started to head towards the lab, Fiona grabbed her arm.

"Don't forget what I told you about the gun. Keep it handy and don't hesitate to use it if you have to and that means on anyone. We've gotten this far and we can't afford any interference or failure."

Jo knew that Fiona included Slattery in her admonition. It was the first time that she felt doubt. If the time came, would she waiver, or, would she see her duties through. The sobering realization was that she would only know the answer to that question if and when the moment came.

The two women separated to carry out their respective tasks. As Jo hurried to the lab building, she quickly checked her watch. Time was quickly passing and the sense of urgency grew.

At first, the black of the moonless night had given her discomfort, but now, it was more like a friend and provided some sense of security and safety. Jo was quickly becoming aware of those things and conditions which assisted survival and of those that did not. She approached the lab building. It was dark and unoccupied as it should have been at that hour of the morning. There was never much going on there of any importance, so, there was no elaborate security system and the door was kept unlocked. Even so, caution would be necessary as she approached. Her gun was at the ready and Fiona's words, to her, were uppermost in her mind. If challenged or even approached, there could be no hesitation in acting. It was an awesome and unfamiliar responsibility.

She approached the building trying to get her mind off the gun which she clutched tightly and on the job at hand. Even though the night air was cool and comfortable, she still felt beads of sweat forming in her forehead and the clamminess of her hands. The front door was just ahead. Questions began racing through her mind. *Where was Slattery? Where was Jack? Was there anyone waiting for her inside the darkened building? What of Fiona?* If her friend failed, for any reason, would she be able to complete their mission.

Fiona was approaching the residence buildings. For some reason, her instincts gave her a sense of foreboding. She was also concerned about the well being of her friend who was thrust into this adventure, willingly, but, somewhat unprepared. But, she, herself, had a job to do and concern for even Jo had to take second place. She was startled by the sound of the door to the main door to the house slamming shut. She froze. Caught out in the open, there was no place or time to hide. She sprawled, as flat as possible, on the ground hoping the darkness would prevent her from being seen. Luck was with her. She stayed motionless so as to not give away her presence. The figure approached her and she could make out the stocky silhouette. It was Jack. She readied her weapon. Firing a shot was the last thing that she wanted to do, lest others, who might be on the premises be alarmed and cause interference. Suddenly Jack altered his path and passed her by not more than ten feet. But, it was obvious that he was preoccupied with getting somewhere to do something as his steps were hurried and not the usual plodding gait she had observed, in her previous encounters with him.

Her relief at avoiding jack was mixed with alarm when she realized that he was headed for the lab building where Jo in the process of planting the two explosive devices. *Damn it,* she thought to herself. It was not entirely unforeseen that they would encounter someone on the compound, even at this hour, but, for it to be Jack at this precise moment and for him to headed toward the lab was the worst of all possibilities. She realized that time would not allow her to deviate from her own task and could only hope that Jo would be able to deal with the situation. If not events would take a complicated and uncertain turn.

You've got to focus, Jo told herself. She arrived at the door of the lab building and found that, as usual, it was unlocked. Opening it slowly and entering the main room, she quickly surveyed the premises using a small flashlight that Fiona had provided. It was just enough illumination to get a fairly good look at the lab, but, not enough to be seen from the outside. Without warning the dead silence of the night was broken by a sound that a chill through her body. Footsteps, heavy and rapid. "Jack", she whispered to herself as the image of the large and dangerous assistant to Slattery filled her mind. *Was he coming after her?* No. If he was on the hunt he would have used more stealth. But, for whatever reason he was only a short distance away. Where to hide? She had to seek cover somewhere in the room and hope that the intruder's visit would be brief. Precious time was rapidly passing.

As silently as possible, she moved away from the entry and crouched behind one of the cabinet's in the room.

The door swung open and a light at the other end of lab went on. She dare not look out and expose herself, but, she could hear the ominous sound of the heavy footsteps heading away from her toward the direction of the lit area. She summoned up the courage to look out from her hiding place. She was right. It was Jack. *But, what in hell was he doing here and more importantly, how long would it take for him to do it? The gun; would she have to use the gun and how long could she wait before making that decision?* She couldn't panic. The situation had to be given more time. *Time, how much time?* Time was more of any enemy than Jack. She checked her watch. It was 3:33 A.M. They had to be out of there in twenty two minutes. She would give Jack three minutes and that was it she decided as fixing her attention on the second hand as it inexorably swept the watch face. Time; nothing could stop it.

Jo crouched in the darkness, watching Jack at one of the computers. He appeared to be downloading something on a disc which stirred her curiosity as she knew of no work in the lab which related to the real purpose of the Foundation. But, there must have been something of value and no doubt Slattery's faithful servant was in full CYA mode. *And what of Slattery? Where was he or had Jack taken care of that loose end himself?* But, she didn't have time for idle speculation. The present situation was reaching a crisis. The wait for Jack was excruciating and tested her self control to its limits. She checked her watch again. It was 3:35 A.M. and counting. As the sweep hand clocked another thirty seconds, she heard the sound of the disc eject. He put it into a case, turned from the computer and walked rapidly out of the building. "Ten seconds to spare", Jo said to herself as she sat there for a moment to compose herself in order to get about her business. She had to move quickly as another precious minute had passed. She set the timers to detonate in twenty four minutes or within seconds of 4:00 A.M. "Close enough", she thought. She placed one under the cabinet where she had hidden and another in a corner at the far side of the room. She hurriedly, but, carefully exited the lab. To her relief, Jack was nowhere to be seen. No doubt he had rushed back to the house to gather up everything that would be of any use to him. Jo knew that, before they left the grounds of the compound, Jack would have to be dealt with. It was a thought which troubled her, but, in some inexplicable way, excited her. It was a feeling of anxiety mingled with anticipation. Her thoughts as to Slattery's outcome were, however, more unsettling.

CHAPTER TWENTY-SIX

Fiona remained at the spot where Jack had passed her. She knew, as she lay there in the dark stillness, that time was more than precious, it was priceless. She would have to react quickly if Jo was discovered as that would fatally compromise the mission. She waited for a minute, calculating that if Jo was initially discovered when Jack entered the lab, it would happen within that time. After that, it would be up to her friend's resourcefulness to deal with the situation. Fiona watched the seconds tick off on her watch. One minute. There was no sound from the lab which would indicate trouble, so, Fiona cautiously continued on to the residence buildings. Upon examining the simple chain link fence which surrounded the simple, brick buildings, she found that there was no particularly elaborate security system to deal with. Access was simple and fast. She realized that the assets that she had brought with her were somewhat limited and insufficient to destroy all of the buildings, completely, although it was unlikely that there was anything contained in these building which would be of much value. Each of the structures had to be accessed, rapidly and without detection. They were small, one story and each was about 1400 square feet, so, time would not be a critical factor, but, stealth would be.

She began making her way through the complex and found that one was completely empty. The second, third and fourth were being utilized for storage and contained new and unused, common lab equipment and spare furniture. She determined that these were unimportant and could be ignored. There could be no doubt, however, from Jo's personal observations, that at least one of the buildings had to be occupied. The questions were, by whom, were they still there and would they pose a threat. If the first two questions were answered in the affirmative, then she knew the answer to the last. All her instincts were telling her that she was now moving into the grim reality of kill or be killed.

Fiona made her way, as fast as caution would allow, to the next building. It was dark, like all of the others. The whole of the compound seemed lifeless, save for Jack. She made it to the entrance and slowly opened the door, stepping inside and aiming her flashlight about, to survey the premises. There was no one in residence, at least not at the moment. The building was equipped with two bedrooms, a bathroom, a medical examination room and a small kitchen. She concluded that this must have been the building where Jo saw the two Asian females.

Fiona scanned her surroundings for the best location to place the charge. The kitchen stove immediately caught her eye. It was gas. She set the timing device and placed it in the oven. For good measure, she extinguished the pilot light and turned the burner knobs on all the way. When the gas was ignited, the destruction would be complete and, with a little luck, the ignition would follow the underground pipes to the other buildings.

For some reason, call it instinct or experience, she had a bad feeling about what she would discover in the last building. Once again, she entered cautiously and once again there was a small kitchen, but, this time two bathrooms. On one side of the building there was a doorway which led into a room which seemed to cover half of the space of the building. She saw and heard nothing and proceeded, gun at the ready. Even before reaching the room, the smell that filled the air told her what she was going to find. Upon entering, she was appalled, but, not surprised at what she discovered. It was a dormitory housing the lab workers, each of them lying peacefully in their beds. But, they would not pose any threat to her on this morning. They were all dead; executed as they slept. They were in all likely drugged and then each was given one bullet in the head. Finally, it was illustrated in the most dramatic and horrific way, just what they were dealing with. But, Fiona had anticipated this from the beginning. She had seen this all played out before at other times, in other places, ruthless plots where anyone and everyone was expendable. Shock or surprise were no longer part of her persona. She liked not to think that Slattery had give the order for this evil, but, the answer to that might never be known. As to the Doctor's fate, that was still to be discovered.

She finished her job at the residence setting two more of the devices and moved on from that scene of grisly carnage. It was a certainty that, before the dawn, greater challenges were to come. Attention now had to be directed to the main house. Fiona approached the building from the side opposite the den which was the only lit room and where she had to presume that some activity was going on. There was no doubt that preparations were being made by Jack to get the hell out and take whatever he could with him. It was a foregone conclusion, to her, that Slattery was not in his plans. It was a good bet that Jack was at least as careless with securing the doors to the house as he was with those of the bunker. She searched the perimeter of the building until she found a likely back entrance. Luck was with her as she tested the door to what appeared to be an isolated part of the house. She slowly turned the knob and cautiously opened the door, tightening her grip on her gun and extending it out in front of her. She found herself in a long narrow hallway, dimly lit from light coming out of a side room. The room must be windowless, she deduced, as she had not detected any light from that wing of the house when she made her search of the perimeter. There was no sound or activity emitting from that area, but, it was now an unknown danger which had to be dealt with. All had to be done without delay as the element of time and its passage remained paramount in her mind. She could see that, approximately twenty feet beyond, the hallway opened into the main area sitting room and beyond that was the den where she was sure that she would find Jack and Slattery.

She approached the room as quietly as possible, pressing herself against the hallway wall next to the doorway. Wheeling her body around, one hundred and eighty degrees, she entered through the portal and assumed a crouched shooting position just inside. It took her a fraction of a second to scan the interior of the space, her line of sight following the barrel of her gun. Suddenly an object caught her attention. It was positioned on a chair. It was lifeless. It was Slattery. The seated body was facing her, with its head leaning over the back of the chair and staring up at the ceiling with open, but, unseeing eyes. Slattery was turned away from the desk in front of which he sat and apparently on which he was doing some work. He was interrupted, turned to look at who was coming through the door and was shot twice in the head. There could be no doubt that the only killer on the premises of the Foundation was Jack and that he had killed the lab employees and Slattery. It provided an odd relief to Fiona to know that her old professor, although having gone astray, had not adopted the evil persona of those he had taken up as colleagues.

Fiona's reflections took only seconds and it was time for her to move on to the ultimate and defining confrontation. She knew that only Jack remained and it was certain that he intended to kill anyone who would pose a present or future inconvenience or threat to him. As she departed the small room that now served as Slattery's final resting place, she wondered as to his final thoughts in that fraction of a second as he faced Jack and became aware that he would be denied his dreams of future greatness in exchange for the finality of death. In that infinitesimal amount of time, she pondered, what thoughts of betrayal, unfulfillment and failure must have gone through his mind. Instead of scientific conquest and professional immortality, he died a sad, desperate and lonely man who had betrayed his colleagues, his academic institution and everything he once stood for. He would not even be an asterisk in the records of scientific history. Once again, the creation had destroyed the creator.

But, she didn't have time to philosophize, as the seconds and minutes sped by. She had to make her way to the main part of the house. As she entered the large sitting room, the place where Slattery had once greeted them with an offering of tea and sandwiches, there now was only Jack who offered nothing but the grim possibility of sudden and violent death.

From her vantage point, the interior of the library was not in her direct line of sight, but, was obstructed by the edge of the wall which comprised part of the archway at the entrance. She had expected to hear some activity. There seemed to be none. All was quiet, much too quiet., but, her options were zero. Perhaps Jack had already left. That would not be good, however it was unlikely. There would be confrontation and during these early morning hours, in these pastoral and seemingly peaceful surroundings, there would be more death. That was a certainty. But facing that prospect was preferable to the possibility of Jack having left with any of the information that he was privy to and which he, no doubt, had gathered together for his own profit, at some later date.

Fiona cautiously made her way into the library, but, found no one. She was, however, alerted by the fact that the computer was on, the screen peering out at her through the darkness with almost a life of its own. There were various files, documents and discs scattered about the desk top. Someone had been feverishly working to download and copy information and likely, it may be that she had interrupted them. No sooner had she given thought to that possibility then, out of the corner of her eye she detected a figure, illuminated by the light of the computer screen and a small desk lamp, reflected in one of the glass doors of a bookshelf on the opposite side of the room. The white lab coat stood out above all else. It was Jack. "Shit"! It was a trap and she walked right into it. Reacting instantly and instinctively, she dove over the top of the desk to seek cover on the other side. For a brief moment there was chaos and desperation. The lamp went crashing to the floor, extinguishing any source of light in the room, except for the glow of the computer as a shot rang out. Fiona felt a searing pain as the bullet hit her even before she hit the floor. The sudden and intense pain from the wound and the impact of hitting the floor caused her to lose her grip on her gun sending it sliding somewhere into the darkness, beyond her reach. The desk was raised on legs giving Fiona some ability to see the figure of the one who had been responsible for the carnage that she had discovered. He stood there illuminated by the computer and did not immediately advance towards her. It was likely that his caution was triggered by his uncertainty of her condition and whether or not she was still armed.

Things were not quiet for very long. Fiona could see the muzzle blast from the darkened entry way as a gunshot rang out. Jack gave out a short grunting sound, dropping his weapon and grasping his right shoulder. Although the light was minimal, Fiona could see the growing dark stain on the sleeve of Jack's lab coat. He leaned his body forward as if in preparation to take a step. Again, a gunshot. This time wide of the mark, the slug imbedding itself in the wall behind where Jack stood. The predator, who had now become the prey, froze in place. Next, a voice.

"Hello, Jack".

Fiona lay still as she recognized the voice of her friend coming from just beyond the entrance to the study. She tried to raise herself up, but, with every move the pain shot through her side and she didn't want to pass out and not be a witness to the drama unfolding before her. She watched as Slattery's former assistant and cold blooded executioner turned haltingly and with some difficulty to face Jo.

"Ah, Doctor Russo."

There was a smirk on Jack's face, but, his voice was flat and without emotion. The fact that he was looking down the barrel of a gun held by someone who was an unknown entity to him seemed not to matter. No doubt his ego fueled by a sociopathic personality allowed him to believe that he could remain in control of the situation as he had, thus far, by elimination all of those who stood in his way. No doubt he had assured himself that his adversary lacked the necessary resolve and that an opportunity would present itself to allow him to kill his way out of the present situation.

There was no response to Jack's sardonic greeting. Jo stepped out of the darkness and into the faint light of the computer screen. There was dead silence as the two locked eyes, Jack showing, for the first time, some discomfort and uncertainty as to how the encounter would end. Fiona saw an expression on Jo's face which was unfamiliar to her that told her exactly how things would end. That moment seemed an eternity but, in fact, only brief seconds passed. At that precise moment, Jo's entire consciousness consisted only of what she saw looking over the barrel of the gun and at the face of her prey. In the last split second of his existence Jack became aware of his fate and that he had underestimated the determination and courage of the woman who stood before him. For Jo, there was no feeling of anger as she thought there might be in facing Peter's killer. There was only a controlled, strong and unswerving resolution to do what had to be done without hesitation. Her sense of mission had now become the controlling force in her life. But, she did take satisfaction in Jack knowing that he was going to die by her hand. That's the least that she could do for Peter. Fiona lay still and tried to control her labored breathing so as not to create a distraction. A gunshot and Jack fell to the floor. Then another gunshot and another, in rapid succession, then a click, click. The five shot snub nose was out of ammunition and the killer who had ruthlessly dispensed so much death was now, himself, nothing more than a lifeless corpse.

"Jo, Jo, over here."

The voice of her friend brought Jo's mind back from that dark and unfamiliar place it had been.

"Fiona, where are you?", she called out, attempting to locate her friend in the darkened room.

"Over here, behind the desk."

Jo tossed away the empty and useless gun. It had done its work. Rushing over to Fiona, she helped her get to her feet. Fiona let out a short grunt..

"Damn, that hurts."

"Where were you hit?"

"On my left side."

"Let me see"

Jo took the flashlight and passes the beam over Fiona's left side, pulling away her jacket and shirt from the area.

"There, I see it. It looks like the bullet grazed your side but didn't penetrate. There's not a lot of bleeding, but, it may have damaged a rib. Let me see what I can do about that."

She went over to Jack, struggled to tear off a good sized piece of his lab coat and removed his belt. She folded the torn piece of cloth and gave it to Fiona.

CHAPTER TWENTY-SIX

"Here, press this to the wound."

With that she put Jack's belt around Fiona's rib cage and cinched it tight, holding the makeshift bandage in place.

"That'll have to do."

"I'll survive. Let's get on with it and get the hell out of here."

As they exited the den, Fiona's attention was briefly called to the no longer menacing Jack lying on the floor.

"Well done", she said, quietly and to herself, but, loud enough for Joe to hear, reflecting on the sight before her.

They went about the business of setting the remaining charge next to Jack's body and under the desk on which sat the computer, assuring complete destruction of any and all pertinent information. As they finished and left, there was a short five minutes to go before the whole place went up. The two hurried out of the confines of the compound leaving behind the remnants of a night, most violent, that neither of them would ever forget. They now had to traverse the back pasture, a daunting task with Fiona in her present condition.

Jo kept up a rapid pace encouraging her friend to keep up with her. She could not afford to slow down for both their sakes. Fiona was suffering. She could not take a deep breath and the constant stabbing pain in her side weakened her. She knew, however, that they had to make it back to the car and get out of the area before the place blew and attracted the whole damned countryside, including the local constabulary. She struggled, trying not to slow the pair down, too much. Then, finally, after what seemed to be forever, they arrived at the Jag. Fiona slumped into the passenger seat and handed Jo the keys.

"Here, you'll have to drive", she indicated, gasping for breath, her face contorted in pain.

Jo jumped into the driver's seat, started the engine and sped away, tires screeching as she headed down the winding road. They had hardly gone more than a mile when they could hear the violence of the multiple explosions and see the sky lighting up behind them. It was obvious that the intensity of the explosions was, in large part, due to the fact that, as Fiona had calculated, the bombs would ignite the underground gas storage tanks, located on the grounds and result in the complete elimination of anything or anyone in the compound. The extent of the destruction plus the fact that the British government, led by its intelligence branch, would mask any and all evidence as to what actually happened that early morning would bring a close to the matter immediately and forever. The only now left to do was to seek help for Fiona and to await the sunrise on a new day.

CHAPTER TWENTY-SEVEN

Three days had passed since the event. Jo was continuing her R & R at Fiona's flat. The effect of her experiences over the past weeks was by far more psychological than physical. Both had been debriefed and Fiona had been checked into a government facility for treatment of her gunshot wound. She was expected to be released within the next five days and Jo was eagerly anticipating her return. For now, there was nothing to do except enjoy the tranquility of Cambridge and the welcome inactivity. That particular evening was unusually cool, even by British standards and there was a dampness in the air from the light, misty rain that had fallen all day and which continued into the dusk. Jo lit a fire, poured a cognac and settled back finding comfort in its warmth and in gazing at the hypnotic dancing of the flames. A sublime feeling of peacefulness washed over her and the events of the Foundation seemed a million years in the past. As she sipped the cognac, the glow of the fire created a buffer between her and the place that she had been three days before. Given this time for reflection, the greater picture began to assemble itself in her thoughts. What had started out, innocently enough, as a sabbatical from work and a trip of three thousand miles across the Atlantic, had become a more profound journey of an infinitely greater distance. It had become an odyssey of the person and the mind. She knew that when Fiona returned there would be questions asked and decisions to be made. *What would her answers be? Would there really be a choice or had the dye already been cast by her actions three nights ago in the darkened study of the main house at the compound?* The answers would come in due time.

The fire and the cognac had done their work. Jo stretched out on the sofa and stared at the ceiling, faintly illuminated from the last of the glowing embers. She had gotten the best sleep of her life over the last three days and tonight would be no exception.

CHAPTER TWENTY-EIGHT

Jo was up at dawn. The day looked to be a pleasant one and warming up, a decided improvement from the previous day. She had not left the flat since returning after the Foundation incident. It was time to get out of her cocoon and resume contact with the outside world. She made her daily call to check on Fiona's condition, finding that she was doing well and would be released within the next couple of days. For now, breakfast tea with Martin would be the order of the day. It would, in all likelihood, be the last time that she would see him.

She freshened up, dressed and looked, with anticipation, at getting back into the world. Stepping out into the fresh air and walking to the college, there was, in her, a heightened awareness of her surroundings and an appreciation of the day, for its own sake, that she had never known before. The blueness of the sky, the clouds, the people of the city, itself. There was the simple, but, glorious state of simply being

285

alive. She found the danger to be intoxicating, but, coming through it and surviving was cathartic and put a person at peace with themselves and the world, at least temporarily. It could truly be addictive with one anxiously anticipating the experience of the next rush.

As she arrived at the entrance, she took a moment to compose herself. So much had happened in her life since her meeting with Martin, when she first arrived. Standing at the doorway to the Porter's office she found Martin engrossed in his daily newspaper. He was holding it up in front of him which allowed her to read the lead headline:

"GAS EXPLOSION DEVASTATES
SERPENTINE FOUNDATION"

Finally the event hit the public media. It was certain that the delay was a result of government to control the story and nothing descriptive could be written until all of the loose ends were tied up. Suspicions might be raised and speculation indulged in and issues never resolved. But, so what? Such is the situation in a number of areas where the government has decided to impose the cloak of absolute secrecy.

Martin sensed her presence, lowered the paper and observed her standing in front of him.

'Tea?", he queried.

It was a word that had become, in practice, a code between them rather than a mere offer of hospitality.

"Please", Jo responded, in a voice that was not much more than a whisper.

Martin busied himself in the ritual that she had observed so many times before, preparing and pouring the brew. He sat down across from her, just observing, for the moment, but, with that familiar, knowing look in his eye as if he could read her innermost thoughts. There was no fooling him as she had discovered over the years, but, although Martin, always the epitome of discretion might let you know, in subtle ways, that he was on to you, he would never be blunt or confrontational.

"Terrible thing that business at the Foundation", he commented.

"It was', Jo responded in an unemotional tone.

"I took some comfort in noting when it happened and was fairly confident that you had avoided the incident without harm."

"I was lucky, I guess."

"Yes, I suppose that you were."

"Did your article, there, go into any details?"

Not much, only that the bodies of Dr. Slattery and his assistant were found or, at least what was left of them. The rest was just rubble and ash; a total loss."

"I'm sorry for the Doctor."

"We all are. But, I always felt that it would come to a bad end. And what about you? Will you be going back to New York?"

"I don't think so. Too many things have changed."

"I expected as much. By the way, I wouldn't say my goodbyes to Doctor Miller, personally, he might be less diplomatic and more inquisitive than I am. I'll just give him your regards."

Jo gave Martin a slight smile. He could read her like a book, but, he would never intrude on her, in a personal way, no matter the circumstances. She knew that it was time to go.

As she got up to leave, Martin came around the desk and kissed her on the cheek.

"I suppose that I am breaking protocol", he commented.

"I have no doubt that the University will survive the breach", Jo responded, giving him a hug, tears starting to well up in her eyes.

Martin was touched by her emotion and was saddened by the realization that this might truly be the last time that he would ever see her.

"You take care of yourself", he said in an earnest voice, his eyes intensely staring into hers.

Jo said nothing more, but, smiled at Martin and bowed her head in acknowledgement of his admonition. She turned and left the office, a feeling of melancholy gripping her as she left another cherished element of her past life, never to be revisited. Her future would be exciting and challenging in entirely new ways, many uncertain and unknown, which added to the anticipation. But, as with everything, there was always a price to pay.

Lost in her thoughts of the past, present and future as she walked the streets of Cambridge, it seemed no time until she was back at the flat. Jo opened the door and as she entered, she stopped abruptly. There before her was a package sitting in the middle of the floor, directly in front of her. A *bomb* was the first thing that crossed her mind given the events of the past few weeks. *No*, she concluded, *that would be pointless and foolish at this stage of the game.*

She cautiously picked up the package, a box approximately two feet by one foot and six inches deep, wrapped in unmarked brown paper save for the designation "Dottoressa" printed in one of the corners. Yes, now she knew who the sender was.

Tearing away the paper, she carefully, but, eagerly opened the box. It contained four items. One was a translucent glass or crystal beaker, of sorts, It was empty. There was a piece of paper, or, parchment, yellow and brittle, which had, obviously, been cut in half as it revealed only part of the unusual DNA strand that Slattery had shown her at the Foundation. There also a very old ship's log, written in French, of a vessel named Mistral, the last entry being in November of 1529 when the ship disembarked from Saint Nazaire. There were no further entries as to the voyage or final port of call.

There was no doubt but that the container had, at one time, held the relic which contained the preserved DNA, a mystery, lost in time until resurrected by Slattery and the Foundation. The sketch of the molecule was the clue and now, incomplete, was useless. The log was the one that Fiona had been told about during her trip to Nantes. Contrary, however, to what they had suspected, it had not been purchased by the Foundation but, rather, by agents of Chan for safekeeping. It now, without the relic or the complete depiction of the DNA molecule, was relegated to nothing more than a souvenir, albeit, a valuable one. The glass vessel, she would keep as a remembrance of her first great adventure and all that had happened to change her life. The log, she would give to Fiona. It was the last fateful voyage of the "Mistral" and the beginning of something that, ultimately, would never be.

She picked up the parchment knowing that this was a message from Piero that the relic had been destroyed and that the same should be done to its remaining record of existence. Jo lit a match and touched it to the corner of the ragged document, throwing it into the fireplace and watched the flame as the parchment was reduced to smoke and cinders until the coded message it contained was no more.

Jo turned her attention to the last item in the box. It was rolled up, but, she recognized it as the unfinished sketch that Pietro had done of her that night in his room over the pub. As she started to unroll it, a small slip of paper dropped out. She reached down and picked it up. The message was brief, simple, powerful and revealing, all at the same time:

"To my Mona Lisa and to the moment."

There was no signature. There didn't have to be.

She spread the picture out on the dining table and studied it. There was an expectation that it would portray her as soft and wistful, reflecting the night that they had spent together. It did not, not at all. True, it illustrated her physical beauty, but the face was strong and set, the eyes intense as if the picture, itself, had a life of it's own and could see those who gazed upon it. He had seen in her what she had not seen in herself, but, came to know by virtue of the events that she had lived through. The sketch, as the note, was not signed or dated, but, at the lower right hand corner it bore the symbol that had been used as the logo for the Foundation, the mark of the Serpentine Curve. These few things confirmed what she had suspected. Collectively they comprised the final piece of the puzzle, that which made the picture whole. Piero was the One. He had been what Slattery and those of the Foundation had been desperately searching for, never realizing that they had found it.

Leonardo di ser Piero da Vinci; that was da Vinci's full name. Leonardo of Piero from Vinci.

Leonardo was from Piero and in a manner of speaking, Piero was now from Leonardo or, rather the DNA contained in the relic that had been spirited from the chateau centuries before. It was lost to history until it reappeared in the young man she had come to know and who would always have a special place in her heart and mind. Thanks to Chan and his network of guardians who had protected the young man and his secret, all of these years, the genie was kept in the bottle.

Pouring herself a glass of wine, she sat down at the table, unable to pull herself away from the portrait. She offered a silent toast to the young man who had, in so short a time, become a huge and permanent part of her life and was so instrumental in the person that she had become or perhaps always was. It was hard to comprehend that she would and could never see him again. Peter, Martin and now Piero, all part of the past except in her mind and soul. She reflected on Peter and Piero, the two relationships that had actually meant anything in her life, one destroyed by the Foundation; one created by it. And what of Piero? Would he lead a life of solitude or would she, someday, be reading about him as a leader in the world of science or medicine, contributing breakthroughs and discoveries for the betterment of humankind; releasing his ever growing knowledge, to the world, in a way so as to not arouse public suspicion as to who and what he really was? But, there was always the terrible alternative that she didn't want to consider, but, had to. Suppose his knowledge and abilities grew to such an extent that he became what he had fought against? Could his uniqueness and total intellectual superiority create in him the same unbridled ambition that led to the destruction of Slattery. Perhaps Chan was not only the guardian of the young man, but, also the protector of humanity. Perhaps, he was there to stop such a thing from happening. The two mysterious and pregnant Asian women added more complexity to the mix. *Would they give birth? If so, would their offspring simply add to the list of failures of the Foundation that had preceded them? Or, would there be success thus unleashing untold danger to the world?* So, the struggle was not over. It never is.

CHAPTER TWENTY-EIGHT

The phone rang. It was Fiona. The conversation was a short one.

"Jo, pack up all of your things, throw them in the Mini and drive up to London tomorrow. I'll meet you in the lounge at the Russell Hotel at 1:00 P.M."

"What's up?"

"You'll see tomorrow. It's too long to go into on the phone."

"And you're OK?"

I'm fine. They did a good job patching me up and I'll be leaving for London this evening."

"Then, I'll see you tomorrow."

" See you then."

CHAPTER TWENTY-NINE

The next morning Jo found herself driving to and arriving in London. She navigated her way through the traffic, finally making her way to the area of Russel Square which was the location of the Hotel Russel, the site of her rendezvous with Fiona. The area was a bustling one with office buildings housing a myriad of professions and commercial ventures. The hotel itself was a friendly and inviting landmark, well known to the business trade. It was a challenge, but, she finally found a place to tuck the Mini away and walk over to hotel. Upon entering the main lobby, she made her way over to the lounge and spotted Fiona as she had expected with a Scotch and a cigarette and seeming none the worse for wear. Her friend waived her over.

"Have a seat and order something up", suggested Fiona.

"It's a bit early isn't it?" responded Jo.

"You'll eventually learn that it's never too early for anything."

Fiona hailed the waitress.

"May I get something for you ladies?"

"I'm fine. What would you like, Jo?"

"Vodka Martini straight up, with a twist, please."

"Very well."

"I though it was too early for you."

"I adapt well."

"Obviously."

"How are you doing with the bullet wound and all", Jo inquired of her friend.

"Fine. They patched me up and gave me some medication. I hardly feel it at all. In a few weeks it'll be nothing more than a learning experience and an unpleasant memory."

"Care to tell me what were up to?"

"I think you've an idea, but let's not get ahead of ourselves. A couple of drinks and a leisurely lunch is just what the doctor ordered, so to speak."

Jo reflected at the irony of what had happened in her life since the last time that she had drinks and lunch with her friend the day after her arrival in England. The two sat across from each other in the now crowded bar, oblivious to those around them, sipping their drinks, barely touching their food, each somewhat lost in their own thoughts. There was some limited conversation about future plans, but, Fiona kept to herself as to what, specifically, was to transpire during the balance of the afternoon.

After about an hour, or so, Fiona checked her watch.

"Drink up. We have an appointment in fifteen minutes."

CHAPTER TWENTY-NINE

"Appointment for what?"

"Patience. I think you'll find it interesting. You might even find it amazing."

They left they hotel and began walking toward one of the generally nondescript buildings located in the square.

"You've brought all of your things with?", queried Fiona.

"Everything's in the Mini."

"Good. Let me have the keys."

"Why?"

"Just a few things we're going to be taking care of."

Jo gave her the keys and stifled any further curiosity.

She eventually found herself on the fifth floor of a building just a stone's throw from the hotel. They walked down the rather austere and unimpressive hallway until they came to a door marked:

HILL & COMPANY
INVESTMENT CONSULTANTS

The entry to the suite was occupied by a receptionist seated behind a rather large and impressive wooden desk. Off to the right and behind a glass partition were two other individuals busying themselves on computers. The plain appearance of the interior of the building belied the opulent appointments of the offices Jo found herself in. In this new world that she occupied, things were never what they initially seemed to be.

"Good morning Miss Clark."

"Good morning Sally."

"And you must be Doctor Russo."

"I'll let Mr. Ward know that you're here."

She announced their arrival over the intercom, got up and escorted them to a back office. As they walked in, the gentleman sitting behind the desk stood up to greet them. He was a tall man with silvery gray thinning hair, a modest handle bar mustache, slightly curled up at each end, a booming voice and sparkling blue eyes with lines at the edges adding to their character all behind gold, wire rimmed glasses. His manner was gregarious, almost jovial and a sharp contrast to the business that he and those under him engaged in.

"Good morning, Fiona."

"Nigel."

"And allow me to extend a special welcome to you Dr. Russo and apologize for our first encounter which was memorable only in it's unpleasantness, but, necessary under the circumstances."

Jo stood in utter amazement. She recognized Nigel Ward as the bothersome passenger on the flight except, this time, with a British accent.

"Will there be anything else?", the receptionist inquired.

"Just take these keys for the Mini, if you would", requested Fiona as she handed them to the young woman.

"Do the surprises ever stop?", commented Jo.

"Not in this business", Ward responded.

"And, what is your business, Mr. Ward?"

"Nigel will do."

"And, what is your business, Nigel?"

"I'm sure that recent events have given you some clue and I would expect that, in popular parlance, you've connected the dots."

"To some extent, but, I still don't have the big picture."

"That's why Fiona set up this meeting, Joanna. May I call you Joanna?"

"Jo will do just fine."

"We're a highly classified, quasi-governmental organization that operates on behalf of the major Western European powers and the United States, but is not directly controlled by them nor do they exercise significant oversight. We report to them, but, do not take our orders from them. We select our operations carefully and in fact you came under our scrutiny the moment that the late Dr. Slattery showed an interest in you, thus, our encounter during the London flight. We maintain a very low profile, both for the accomplishment of any mission and for the protection of our operatives in the field."

"You didn't do so well with Peter Simpson", interrupted Jo.

Ward paused.

"That was a rare and unfortunate incident, but, in light of your recent experiences, I'm sure you've become well aware that this is a dangerous and sometimes deadly business and the loss of one of our own from time to time is an unavoidable and nasty byproduct of what we do."

Jo shot a silent glance at Fiona.

Ward continued.

"We deal in the interruption of the best laid plans of those forces in the world who seek to destroy our civilization and remake it according to their own sinister visions. In the past, this has meant, primarily, with matters concerning the world's oil supply, nuclear material and other weapons of mass destruction and most recently the world wide terrorist threat. All of these, as serious a threat as they pose, have become run of the mill, almost passé, for us. Although we're still very actively involved in these areas we've entered into the brave new world of science, genetics, focusing our attention and resources on anything and everything bad that can be done by those who would choose to misapply them. Some peripheral information has even made it into the mainstream news. Dolly, the cloned sheep and embryonic research is fairly common knowledge, but, those are only indicators of the possibilities. On ever increasing occasions statements are made which raise a red flag. Here in the U.K., itself, organizations advance the notion of inter-species clones and of introducing human DNA into animals or developing human-animal embryos, always with the suspect admonition that such would never be implanted in either a human or animal for the full period of gestation, perhaps, creating the dream of every tyrant, that of the sub-human super soldier. On the present state of affairs, as to such things, we are presently developing actionable intelligence. But, of one thing we are certain. If it can be done, it will be done. There are these and other things which are so top secret that they cannot presently be mentioned even between us in the confines of this office to which we address ourselves."

"Sort of protecting the world against itself?", Jo mused.

"You could say that even though it might have a tinge of arrogance about it. But, I think you've got the basic picture and to put it bluntly, we'd like you to join us. Your scientific background would be invaluable both as a cover an in giving you the much needed expertise that will be required in tour duties. Our most recent endeavor in which you found yourself enmeshed has shown us, conclusively, that you have the personal and psychological qualities that we're looking for."

"So, in a very real way, I was being tested."

"I won't deny that."

"Is manipulation also part of your stock-in-trade?", Jo asked in a decidedly irritated tone.

"It is one of the arrows in our quiver and we use it when we have to. Our business is a serious", Ward paused, "no, let me rephrase that; a grave one. We must accomplish what we undertake and we do everything possible to protect our people, but, they are expendable."

"People such as Peter?"

"Ward looked her in the eye and silently nodded in the affirmative.

"Well, I appreciate the candor."

"We receive no benefit from being deceptive when we choose to recruit someone such as yourself. We're asking you to make, what up until now, is probably the most important decision of your life. You have a month to reflect on what you've been through and what I've told you. If you decide in the affirmative, you can report back to this office within that time. If you choose not to join us and I don't see you within that one month time period, our paths shall not cross again and you will have to sever all relationships with Fiona. I have faith in your character and integrity in not revealing what you have learned about us over the past month, otherwise, you wouldn't be here in this office sitting across from me." He grinned slightly. "I'm sure that you've turned over in your mind that if you did, however, become a danger to our operation, that you would be dealt with."

"I've given that due consideration."

"Good."

Jo sat there silently her eyes transfixed on Ward, but not seeing him. She was alone with her thoughts; her thoughts of Peter and those friends during that awful day in New York City that gave evidence of the existence of the barbaric hordes of many races, nationalities and ideologies whose mission it is to eradicate all that she treasured in their unquenchable thirst for conquest and power to turn the earth into the hell that they envision. And what of Piero, the young man whose infinite knowledge would be lost to humanity in order that it be kept from the hands of the sinister forces that she would be fighting against? What would Peter want her to do? There was no need to wait a month. The answer was clear as clear could be. She looked Ward in the eye and with a determined tone in her voice gave him his decision, there and then.

CHAPTER TWENTY-NINE

"Yes."

"Splendid", exclaimed Ward, barely being able to hide his exuberance at her decision. "Let me assure you that you will not regret your decision."

Fiona said nothing, but, gave her friend an approving smile.

"I don't believe that we have anything more", announced Ward, bringing their meeting to an abrupt close.

"We've taken care of advising your employer in the states that you won't be returning. Also, in conjunction with your association with our group a bank account of a substantial amount will be opened for you and replenished as you need it. Fiona will give you the details. And by the way, Sicily is quite lovely this time of year.

Jo nodded in acknowledgement and marveled with some discomfort as to how much they really knew about even her most private matters and the efficiency with which they dealt with them.

The two women made their way back to the busy London streets and walked to the spot where Jo had parked the Mini. It was gone.

"That's strange", she exclaimed, surprised at not finding the familiar red car, "I could have sworn this is where I parked."

"It is", Fiona responded.

"But, what's this."

Jo stood there looking at a new satin gray Maserati coupe.

"Let's just say that it's a gift from Nigel. He anticipated your answer and decided that this would be a more fitting vehicle for one of his operatives. He suggested a getaway for the both of us would be a good idea. I know I can certainly use one. Your luggage was transferred from the Mini and I packed some of my stuff for a trip to the continent. Sicily will be our destination and Nigel arranged for use of a cottage, next to a thirteenth century monastery. The most threatening thing we'll encounter is the livestock and the most we'll have to concern ourselves with is drinking too much wine and eating too much pasta."

Fiona handed Jo the car keys and the two began their much delayed journey.

As they made their way to the Tunnel Train, which would take them to the continent, Fiona gave Jo some additional background and details on the organization and it's mission. Nothing more was mentioned as to the ordeal they both had recently endured.

They finally settled in on the train and were leaving England behind them on their way to some welcome and much needed peace and serenity. Jo could picture herself reclining on a grassy hillside, soaking up the sun while sipping a glass of local red, she hoped. There was now the reality of Nigel Ward who would be an unseen, but, constant presence able to call her into service at any time. Still, she was confident that she would be left alone, at least for as reasonable period of time.

Again, her mind drifted to thoughts of Pietro. There was a sadness in her that he would no longer be a part of her life. Her personal feelings were mingled with the realization that it would not nor could it ever be revealed what knowledge and insight was contained in his incredible mind. What he was would always be kept the deepest secret. The truth was a danger to him, to those around him and to the human race. He, himself, better than anyone else, knew that. No, he would have to lead a life of total anonymity; a virtual recluse. His intellect and all that it was capable of, lost to the world forever.

She looked across at Fiona who had drifted off into a peaceful sleep partly from delayed exhaustion and partly from her medication. Within the space of the past month their lives had intersected in a way that she could never have imagined. They had become infinitely closer than they had ever been during their university days and the ensuing years. Jo pondered the present and the future and where her life would be going in light of events of the moment and the recent profound changes that she had undergone. She had lost much, but, she had gained much. She was still trying to measure the balance. Life and attitude was always a matter of personal perspective. She had become keenly aware of what most people fail to realize until it's too late. There is only now. There is only the moment in which each of us presently exist. The rest is so much surplusage. What's past is past and what the future holds, in any meaningful way, is left to forces far greater than any one individual. But, that was fine with her. She had never felt more alive. She was where she had wanted to be, for a very long time; no longer an observer, but, a player in matters that would impact the direction that human civilization would take. Looking at her sleeping friend and reflecting on the meeting with Nigel Ward, it was becoming more clear to her. She had abandoned her past and become one of them. There was no turning back.

CPSIA information can be obtained
at www.ICGtesting.com
Printed in the USA
LVOW03s2248090218
566053LV00001B/54/P